Marx Machiavelli Chesterton Emerson Joyce
Abbott Hardy Montaigne Cooper Austen
Defoe Melville Haggard Hugo
Christie Carroll Eliot Grimm
Stoker Molière
Wilde Maupassant Byron
Engels Schiller
Garnett Einstein Fitzgerald Smith
Goethe Hawthorne Kafka
Cotton Dostoyevsky Hall
Baum Kipling Doyle Willis
Leslie Dumas Henry Nietzsche
Flaubert Turgenev Balzac
Stockton Vatsyayana Crane
Burroughs Whitman Verne
Curtis Tocqueville Gogol Vinci
Homer Widger Tolstoy Busch
Darwin Thoreau
Potter Freud Zola Twain Plato Scott
Lawrence
Kant Jowett Stevenson Dickens
Andersen Cervantes Burton Hesse Harte
London Descartes
Poe Aristotle Wells Voltaire
Hale James Hastings Cooke
Bunner Shakespeare
Richter Chambers Irving
Doré Swift Dante Chekhov da Shaw Wodehouse Benedict Alcott
Pushkin
Newton

tredition®

tredition was established in 2006 by Sandra Latusseck and Soenke Schulz. Based in Hamburg, Germany, tredition offers publishing solutions to authors and publishing houses, combined with worldwide distribution of printed and digital book content. tredition is uniquely positioned to enable authors and publishing houses to create books on their own terms and without conventional manufacturing risks.

For more information please visit: www.tredition.com

TREDITION CLASSICS

This book is part of the TREDITION CLASSICS series. The creators of this series are united by passion for literature and driven by the intention of making all public domain books available in printed format again - worldwide. Most TREDITION CLASSICS titles have been out of print and off the bookstore shelves for decades. At tredition we believe that a great book never goes out of style and that its value is eternal. Several mostly non-profit literature projects provide content to tredition. To support their good work, tredition donates a portion of the proceeds from each sold copy. As a reader of a TREDITION CLASSICS book, you support our mission to save many of the amazing works of world literature from oblivion. See all available books at www.tredition.com.

Project Gutenberg

The content for this book has been graciously provided by Project Gutenberg. Project Gutenberg is a non-profit organization founded by Michael Hart in 1971 at the University of Illinois. The mission of Project Gutenberg is simple: To encourage the creation and distribution of eBooks. Project Gutenberg is the first and largest collection of public domain eBooks.

The Ghost of Guir House

Charles Willing Beale

Imprint

This book is part of TREDITION CLASSICS

Author: Charles Willing Beale
Cover design: Buchgut, Berlin – Germany

Publisher: tredition GmbH, Hamburg - Germany
ISBN: 978-3-8424-3316-8

www.tredition.com
www.tredition.de

THE GHOST OF GUIR HOUSE

By

CHARLES WILLING BEALE

1897

1

When Mr. Henley reached his dingy little house in Twentieth Street, a servant met him at the door with a letter, saying:

"The postman has just left it, sir, and hopes it is right, as it has given him a lot of trouble."

Mr. Henley examined the letter with curiosity. There were several erased addresses. The original was:

"*Mr. P. Henley, New York City.*"

Scarcely legible, in the lower left-hand corner, was:

"*Dead. Try Paul, No. –, W. 20th.*"

Being unfamiliar with the handwriting, Mr. Henley carried the letter to his room. It was nearly dark, and he lighted the gas, exchanged the coat he had been wearing for a gaudy smoking jacket, glancing momentarily at the mirror, at a young and gentlemanly face with good features; complexion rather florid; hair and moustache neither fair nor dark, with reddish lights.

Seating himself upon a table directly under the gas, he proceeded with the letter. Evidently the document was not intended for him, but it proved sufficiently interesting to hold his attention.

GUIR HOUSE, 16TH SEPT., 1893.

MY DEAR MR. HENLEY:

Although we have never met, I feel sure that you are the man for whom I am looking, which conclusion has been reached after carefully considering your letters. Why have I taken so long to decide? Perhaps I can answer that better when we meet. Do not forget that the name of our station is the same as that of the house—Guir. Take the evening train from New York, and you will be with us in old Virginia next day, not twenty-four hours. I shall meet you at the station, where I shall go every day for a month, or until you come. You will know me because—well, because I shall probably be the only girl there, and because I drive a piebald horse in a cart with red wheels—but how shall I know you? Suppose you carry a red handkerchief in your hand as you step upon the platform. Yes, that will do famously. I shall look for the red silk handkerchief, while you look for the cart with gory wheels and a calico horse. What a clever idea! But how absurd to take precautions in such a desolate country as this. I shall know you as the only man stopping at Guir's, and you will know me as the only woman in sight.

Of course you will be our guest until you have proved all things to your satisfaction, and don't forget that I shall be looking for you each day until I see you. Meanwhile believe me

Sincerely yours,

DOROTHY GUIR.

"Devilish strange letter!" said Henley, turning the sheet over in an effort to identify the writer. But it was useless. Dorothy Guir was as complete a myth as the individual for whom her letter was intended. Oddly enough, the man's last name, as well as the initial of his first, were the same as his own; but whether the P. stood for Peter, Paul, or Philip, Mr. Henley knew not, the only evident fact being that the letter was *not* intended for himself.

Reading the mysterious communication once more, the young man smiled. Who was Dorothy Guir? Of course she was Dorothy Guir, but what was she like? At one moment he pictured her as a charming girl, where curls, giggles, and blushes were strangely intermingled with moonlight walks, rope ladders, and elopements. At the next, as some monstrous female agitator; a leader of Anarchists and Nihilistic organizations, loaded with insurrectionary documents for the destruction of society. But the author was inclined to playfulness; incompatible with such a character. He preferred the former picture, and throwing back his head while watching the smoke from his cigarette curl upward toward the ceiling, Mr. Paul Henley suddenly became convulsed with laughter. He had conceived the idea of impersonating the original Henley, the man for whom the letter had been written. The more he considered the scheme, the more fascinating it became. The girl, if girl she were, confessed to never having met the man; she would therefore be the more easily deceived. But she was expecting him daily, and should not be disappointed. Love of adventure invested the project with an irresistible charm, and Mr. Henley determined to undertake the journey and play the part for all he was worth. It is true that visions of embarrassing complications occasionally presented themselves, but were dismissed as trifles unworthy of consideration.

It was still early in October, while Miss Guir's communication had been dated nearly three weeks before. Had she kept her word? Had she driven to the station every day during those weeks? Mr. Henley jumped down from the table, exclaiming:

"Yes, Miss Dorothy, I will be with you at once, or as soon as the southern express can carry me." A moment later he added: "But I shall glance out of the car window first, and if I don't like your looks, or if you are not on hand, why in that event I shall simply continue my journey. See?"

But another question presented itself. Where was Guir Station? The lady had mentioned neither county nor county town, evidently taking it for granted that the right Henley knew all about it, which he doubtless did; but, since he was dead, it was awkward to consult him, especially about a matter which was manifestly a private affair of his own. But where was Guir? In all the vast State of Virginia, how was he to discover an insignificant station, doubtless unknown to New York ticket agents, and perhaps not even familiar to those living within twenty miles of it? Paul opened the atlas at the "Old Dominion," and threw it down again in disgust. "A map of the infernal regions would be as useful," he declared. However important Guir might be to the Guirs, it was clearly of no importance to the world. But the following day the Postal Guide revealed the secret, and the railway officials confirmed and located it. Guir was situated in a remote part of the State, upon an obscure road, far removed from any of the trunk lines. Mr. Henley purchased his ticket, resolved to take the first train for this *terra incognita* of Virginia.

The train drew up at the station. Yes, there was the piebald horse, and there was the cart with the gory wheels, and there—yes, certainly, there was Dorothy, a slender, nervous-looking girl of twenty, standing at the horse's head! Be she what she might, politically, socially, or morally, Mr. Henley decided at the first glance that she would do. With a flourish of his crimson handkerchief he stepped out upon the platform. "Rash man! You have put your foot in it," he soliloquized, "and you may never, *never* be able to take it out again." But he could as soon have passed the open doors of Paradise unheeded as Dorothy Guir at that moment.

"Mr. Henley! So glad!" said the girl in recognition of the young man's hesitating and somewhat prolonged bow. "He's a little afraid of the engine," she continued, alluding now to the horse, "so if you will jump in and take the reins while I hold his head— "

Paul tossed in his bag and satchels, and then jumping in himself gathered up the reins, while the girl stood at the animal's head.

Although Mr. Henley had hoped to find an attractive young woman awaiting him at the station, he was surprised to discover that his most sanguine expectations were exceeded. Here was no blue-stocking, or agitator, or superannuated spinster, but a graceful young woman, rather tall and slight, with blue eyes, set with dark lashes that intensified their color. Her complexion, although slightly freckled, charmed by its wholesomeness; and her hair, which shone both dark and red, according as the light fell upon it, seemed almost too heavy for the delicate head and neck that supported it. Although not strictly beautiful, she had one of those intelligent and responsive faces that are often more attractive than mere perfection of feature and form.

"It does seem funny that you are here at last!" she said, when seated beside him with the reins in her hand.

"It does indeed!" answered Paul, with a suspicion that he was a villain and ought to be kicked. For a moment he scowled and bit his mustache, hesitating whether to make a clean breast of the deception or continue in the role he had assumed. Alas, it was no longer of his choosing. He had commenced with a lie, which he now found it impossible to repudiate. No, he could not insult this girl by telling her the truth. That surely was out of the question.

Miss Guir touched the horse with the whip, and the station was soon out of sight. They ascended a long hill with gullies, bordered by worm fences and half-cultivated fields. Such improvements as there were appeared in a state of decay, and, so far as Henley could see, the country was uninhabited. Presently the road entered a wood and became carpeted with pine tags, over which they trotted noiselessly. Where were they going? Dorothy had not spoken since starting, and Paul was too much disconcerted to continue the conversation. He hoped she would speak first, and yet dreaded anything which it seemed at all probable she would say. The novelty was intense, but the agony was growing. At last, without looking at him, she said:

"You haven't told me why you never answered my last letter. You know we have been expecting you for ages."

Paul coughed, hesitated, and then resolved to tell a part of the truth, which is often more misleading than the blackest lie.

"I—I did not get it," he answered, "until a day or two ago."

Miss Dorothy looked surprised.

"Strange!" she said; "but, after all, I had my misgivings, for I never could believe that a letter like that would reach its destination. But you know you told me—"

"Yes, I know I did," interrupted Paul. "You were perfectly right. You see I got it at last, and 'all's well that ends well!'"

"Not necessarily; because if you are as careless about other matters as this, why—I may have—that is, *we* may have to part before really knowing each other, and do you know, *I* should be awfully sorry for that."

Although she laughed a quick, nervous laugh, the words were uttered as if really meant. Paul suffered, and tried to think of something non-committal—something which, while not exposing his ignorance of the real Henley's business, might induce the girl to explain the situation; but no leading question presented itself. He thought he could be happy if he could but divert the conversation from its present awkward drift.

There was a quaintness about the young lady's costume that reminded Henley of an old portrait. Evidently her attire had been modeled after that of some remote ancestor, but it was picturesque and singularly becoming, and Paul found it difficult to avoid staring in open admiration. Inwardly he concluded that she was a "stunner," but in no ordinary sense; and despite the novel and somewhat embarrassing situation, he was conscious of a fascination not clearly accounted for. Thoughts of the defunct Henley, with his store of inaccessible knowledge, were discouraging; but then the memory of the girl's smiles was reassuring; and, come what might, Paul determined to represent his namesake as creditably as possible.

The loneliness of the country road begot a spirit of confidence, so that Miss Guir soon appeared in the light of an old friend, to deceive whom was sacrilege. Mr. Henley realized the enormity of his conduct each time he glanced at her pretty face, but had not the courage to undeceive her. And why should he? Was not Dorothy happy? "Would it be right," he argued, "to upset the girl's tranquillity for a whim, for a scruple of his own, which had come too late, and which, for his as well as the girl's peace of mind, had better not have come at all? No, he would continue as he had begun. Doubtless he would be discovered ere long, but would not anticipate the event."

The forest was beginning to take on its autumnal tints, but Mr. Henley's conscience barred his thorough enjoyment of the scene. They followed the bank of a brook where wild ivy and rhododendrons clustered. They climbed steep places and descended others, and crossed a little river, where rocks and a rushing torrent made the ford seem dangerous. It was lonely, but exquisitely beautiful, and the mountain ridges closed about them on every hand.

The twilight was rapidly giving way to the soft illumination of a full moon; and it was not until Paul noticed this, that he began to ask himself, "Where are we going?" He could not put the question to the girl, and expose his ignorance of a matter which he might reasonably be supposed to know.

After a prolonged silence, Henley ventured to observe that he had never been in the State of Virginia before, hoping that the remark might lead to some information from his driver; but she only looked at him with a wondering expression, and after a minute, with eyebrows lifted, said:

"And I have never been out of it."

Paul would have liked to pursue the conversation, but did not know how to do it. So far from gaining any information, he felt that he was sinking deeper in the mire. "After all," he reflected, "there are worse things in life than being run away with by a pretty girl, even if one doesn't happen to know exactly where she is taking him, and even if she doesn't happen to know exactly whom she is taking." He stretched out his feet and leaned back, resigned to his fate.

Not a house had been passed in more than a mile. The road was deserted, and Paul's interest in future developments steadily growing.

Suddenly there was a terrible crash, and Mr. Henley's side of the cart collapsed. Dorothy drew up the horse and exclaimed:

"There! It is the spring. I was afraid it would break!"

"Too much weight on my side, Miss Guir," said Paul, jumping to the ground.

"It is not that; it was weak; and I should have remembered to place your luggage on my side. It is too unfortunate."

"What are we to do?" inquired Henley.

"It is difficult to say. We are miles from home, and the road is rough."

She was examining the broken spring by the uncertain light, and seemed perplexed.

"Can I not lead the horse while we walk?" suggested Paul.

"We could, but the break is too bad. I fear the body of the cart will fall from the axle. But stop; there is one thing I can do. There is a smith about half a mile from here, upon another road, which leaves this about a hundred yards ahead. I will drive on alone to the shop, and, although it is late, I feel sure the man will do the work for me.

You, Mr. Henley, will wait here for the stage, which will be due directly. Tell the driver to put you off at the Guir Road, where you can wait until I come along to pick you up. The distance is not great, and I will follow as quickly as possible."

She was off before he had time to answer, leaving him standing by the roadside, waiting for the promised coach. It was not long before the rumbling of a heavy vehicle was heard, and but a few minutes more when an antiquated stage with four scrubby horses emerged from the shadow of a giant oak into the open moonlight, scarce fifty yards away. Mr. Henley hailed the driver, who stopped, and looked at him as if frightened. The man was a Negro, and, when convinced that it was nothing more terrible than a human being who had accosted him, smiled generously and invited him to a seat on the box.

"I 'lowed yer was a *hant*" observed the man, by way of opening the conversation, when Paul had handed up his bags and taken his place on top. Henley lighted a cigar, and the cumbersome old vehicle moved slowly forward.

Their way now lay through a beautiful valley, beside a picturesque stream, tunneling its course through wild ivy and magnificent banks of calmia, and under the wide spreading limbs of pines and hemlocks. The country appeared to be a wilderness, and Paul could not help feeling that the real world of flesh and ambition lay upon the other side of the ridge, now far behind. The night was superb, but the road rough, so that the horses seldom went out of a walk. Presently the driver drew up his animals for water, and Henley took the opportunity to question him.

"Do you know these Guirs where I am going?" he inquired.

The man paused in the act of dipping a pail of water, and seemed puzzled. Thinking he had not understood, Paul repeated the question, when the man dropped the bucket, and staring at him with a look of horror, said:

"Boss, is you uns in airnest?"

Henley laughed, and told him that he thought he was, adding that Miss

Guir was a friend of his.

"Now I knows you uns is jokin', 'case dey ain't got no friends in dis 'ere country."

"But I am a stranger!" argued Paul.

"Well, sah, it ain't for de likes o' me to argify wid you uns, but ef you wants to know whar de house is, I kin show it to you; leastways I kin show you de road to git dar."

"That's it; but tell me, don't the people about here like the Guirs?"

"Boss, ef dey's frens o' yourn, I reckon you knows all about 'em; maybe more'n I kin tell you, and I reckon it's saiftest for me to keep my mouf shet tight!"

"Why so? Explain. Surely Miss Guir is a very charming young lady."

"I reckon she be, boss; dough for my part I ain't nebber seed her. Folks says as how it ain't good luck when she trabels on de road."

"What do you mean? Are any of her people accused of crime?"

"Not as ever I heerd on, sir."

"Then explain yourself. Speak!"

But not another word was to be gotten out of the man. He was like one grown suddenly dumb, save for the power of an occasional shout to his horses. A mile beyond this the driver drew up his team, and turning abruptly, said:

"You see dat paf?"

After peering doubtfully through the moonlight into the black shadows beyond, Paul thought he discerned the outline of a narrow wood road, and placing a tip in the man's hand, picked up his satchel and climbed down to the ground.

"Tank 'ee, sir, and de Lawd take keer o' you when you gets to de Guirs'," called the driver, as he cracked his whip and drove away, leaving Mr. Henley standing by the roadside listening to the retreating wheels of the coach. The forest was dense, and the moonlight, struggling through the tree-tops, fell upon the ground in patches, adding to the obscurity. Henley seated himself upon a fallen tree, to await the arrival of the cart. Although quite as courageous as the average of men, he could not help a slight feeling of apprehension concerning the outcome of his enterprise. Of course, he knew nothing about these people; but the girl was prepossessing and refined to an unusual degree. It seemed impossible that she could be acting as a decoy for unworthy ends. He laughed at the thought, and at the fun he would some day have in recounting his fears to her, and at her imaginary explanation of the driver's silly talk. At the same time he examined his revolver, which he kept well concealed, despite the law, in the depths of a convenient pocket.

When twenty minutes had passed, he began to grow impatient for the girl's arrival, and, when half an hour was up, started down the road to meet her. Scarcely had he done so when the sound of approaching wheels greeted his ears, and directly after Miss Guir was in full view.

"I hope you have been successful," Paul asked as she drew up beside him.

"Quite," answered the girl; "indeed, they put in a new spring for me; and we can now drive home without fear."

"Do you know, I have been half frightened," said Paul, climbing into the cart beside her.

"And about what, pray?"

"Absurd nonsense, of course; but the old man who drove the coach talked the most idiotic stuff when I asked him about your people. Indeed, from his manner, I believe he was afraid of you."

Miss Guir did not laugh, nor seem in the least surprised. She only drew a long breath and said:

"Very likely!"

"But why should he be?" persisted Henley.

"It does seem strange," said the girl, pathetically, "but many people are."

"I am sure I should never be afraid of you," added Paul, confidentially.

"I hope not; and am I anything like what you expected?" she asked with languid interest.

"Well, hardly—at least, you are better than I expected—I mean that you are better—looking, you know."

He laughed, but the girl was silent. There was nothing trivial in her manner, and she drove on for some minutes, devoting herself to the horse and a careful scrutiny of the road, whose shadows, ruts, and stones required constant attention. Presently, in an open space, bathed in a flood of moonlight, she turned toward him and said:

"I can not reciprocate, Mr. Henley, by saying that you are better than I expected, for I expected a great deal; I also expected to like you immensely."

"Which I hope you will promptly conclude to do," Paul added, with a twinkle in his eyes, which was lost on his companion, in her endeavor to urge the horse into a trot.

"No," she presently answered, "I can conclude nothing; for I like you already, and quite as well as I anticipated."

"I'm awfully glad," said Henley, awkwardly, "and hope I'll answer the purpose for which I was wanted."

"To be sure you will. Do you think that I should be bringing you back with me if I were not quite sure of it?"

He had hoped for a different answer—one which might throw some light upon the situation—but the girl was again quiet and introspective, without affording the slightest clew to her thoughts. How did it happen that he had proved so entirely satisfactory? Perhaps, then, after all, the original Henley was not so important a personage as he had imagined. But Paul scarcely hoped that his identity would remain undiscovered after arriving at the young lady's home; then, indeed, he might expect to be thrown upon his mettle to make things satisfactory to the Guirs.

They had been jogging along for half a mile, when, turning suddenly through an open gateway, they entered a private approach. Paul exclaimed in admiration, for the road was tunneled through such a dense growth of evergreens that the far-reaching limbs of the cedars and spruce pines brushed the cart as they passed.

"Romantic!" Henley exclaimed, standing up in the vehicle to hold a branch above the girl's head as she drove under it. The little horse tossed the limbs right and left as he burrowed his way amongst them.

"Wait until you know us better," said Dorothy, dodging a hemlock bough; "you might even come to think that several other improvements could be made beside the trimming out of this avenue; but Ah Ben would as soon cut off his head as disturb a single twig."

"Who?" inquired Paul.

"Ah Ben."

Mr. Henley concluded not to push his investigations any further for the present, taking refuge in the thought that all things come to him who waits. He had no doubt that Ah Ben would come along with the rest.

A sudden turn, and an old house stood before them. It was built of black stones, rough as when dug from the ground more than a century before. At the farther end was a tower with an open belfry, choked in a tangle of vines and bushes, within which the bell was dimly visible through a crust of spiders' webs and birds' nests. Patches of moss and vegetable mold relieved the blackness of the stones, and a venerable ivy plant clung like a rotten fish-net to the wall. It was a weird, yet fascinating picture; for the house, like a rocky cliff, looked as if it had grown where it stood. Parts of the building were crumbling, and decay had laid its hand more or less heavily upon the greater part of the structure. All this in the mellow light of the moon, and under the peculiar circumstances, made a scene which was deeply impressive.

"This is Guir House," said Dorothy, drawing up before the door. "Now don't tell me how you like it, because you don't know. You must wait until you have seen it by daylight."

She threw the reins to a stupid-looking servant, who took them as if not quite knowing why he did so. She then made a signal to him with her hands, and jumped lightly to the ground.

"Down, Beelzebub!" called Dorothy to a huge dog that had come out to meet them, while the next instant she was engaged in exchanging signals with the servant, who immediately led the horse away, followed by the dog.

"Why does the boy not speak?" inquired Paul, considerably puzzled by what he had seen.

"*Because he is dumb,*" answered the girl, leading the way up to the door.

Paul carried his luggage into the porch where he saw that Dorothy's eyes were fixed upon him with that strange *quizzo-critical* gaze, with lids half closed and head tilted, which he had observed once before, and which he could not help thinking gave her a very aristocratic bearing.

"You should carry one of those long-handled lorgnettes," he suggested, "when you look that way."

"And why?" she asked quite innocently.

"To look at me with," answered Henley, hoping to induce a smile, or a more cheery tone amid a gloom which was growing oppressive. But Miss Guir simply led the way to the great hall door, which was built of heavy timber, and studded with nail-heads without. As the cumbersome old portal swung open, Paul could not help observing that it was at least two inches thick, braced diagonally, and that the locks and hinges were unusually crude and massive. He followed Miss Guir into the hall, with a slight foreboding of evil which the memory of the stage driver's remark did not help to dispel.

2

There are few men who would not have felt uncomfortable in the peculiar situation in which Mr. Henley now found himself, although, perhaps, he was as little affected as any one would have been under the circumstances. It was impossible now to retreat from the part assumed, and he resolved to carry it out to the best of his ability, never doubting for an instant that the deception would be discovered sooner or later.

Following Miss Guir across the threshold of her mysterious home, Henley entered a hall which was by far the most extraordinary he had ever beheld, and he paused for a moment to take in the scene. The room was nearly square, with a singular staircase ascending from the left. Upon the side opposite the door was a huge chimney, where a fire of logs was burning in an enormous rough stone fireplace, doubly cheering after their long drive through the cool October evening. A brass lamp of antique design, with perforated shade of the same material, was suspended from the ceiling, and helped illumine this strange apartment. From each end of the mantelpiece an immense high-backed sofa projected into the room, cushioned and padded, and looking as if built into its present position with the house. The walls were covered with odd portraits, whose frames were crumbling in decay, and the window curtains adorned with fairy scenes and mythological figures. The ceiling was crossed with heavy beams of oak, black with the smoke of a century; and the stairway upon the left was also black, but ornamented with a series of rough panels, upon each of which was painted a human face, giving it a somewhat fantastic appearance. Paul could not help glancing above, toward the mysterious regions with which this eccentric stairway communicated. An antique sofa, studded with brass nails, exhibited upon its towering back a picture of Tsong Kapa reclining under the tree of a thousand images at the Llamasary of Koomboom. There were scenes which were evidently intended to be historical, but there were others which were wild and inexplicable. The quaintness of the room was intensified by the flickering fire and the shafts of yellow light emitted through the perforations of the lamp.

A faint aromatic odor hung upon the air, possibly due to a pile of balsam logs in a corner near the chimney. Over all was the unmistakable evidence of age, and of a nature at once barbaric, eccentric, and artistic. Who had conceived and executed this extraordinary apartment? And what were the people like who called the place their home? Paul stood aghast and wondered as he inwardly propounded these questions.

The girl led the way to the fire, and, seating herself upon one of the sofas described, invited Paul to the opposite place. His bewilderment was intense, and with a lingering gaze at the oddities surrounding him, he accepted the invitation. Not another soul had been seen since he entered. Did the girl live alone? It seemed incredible; and yet where were her people?

Dorothy pulled off her gloves and warmed her fingers before the cheerful blaze, and then stood eying with evident satisfaction the costly gems with which they were loaded. The light seemed to shine directly through her delicate palms, and to fall upon her face and hair and quaint old-fashioned costume with singular effect. There was something so bizarre and yet so spirituelle in her appearance that Henley could not help observing in what perfect harmony she seemed with her environment. It was some minutes before either of them spoke—Paul loth to express his surprise for fear of betraying a lack of knowledge he might possibly be expected to possess, while Dorothy, in an apparent fit of abstraction, had evidently forgotten her guest and all else, save the cheerful fire before her. Presently she withdrew her eyes from their fixed stare at the flames, and, looking at Paul, said:

"You must be hungry."

There was something so incongruous with his surroundings and recent train of thought in the girl's sudden remark that Henley could not help laughing.

"One would scarcely expect to eat in such a remarkable home as yours, Miss Guir," he replied, looking into her earnest eyes, and wondering if she ordinarily dined alone.

"Nevertheless, we will in an hour," she answered, "and I shall expect you to have an excellent appetite after our long drive."

Paul wanted to ask about the members of her family, but thought it wisest to say nothing for the present. Surely they would appear in due season, for it was impossible the girl could live alone in so large a house, and without natural protection; and so he simply made a further allusion to the apparent age and great picturesqueness of the building.

"Yes," said Dorothy, again gazing into the fire, "it is old—considerably more than a hundred years. It was built in the Colonial days, when things were rougher and good work more difficult to obtain."

"But surely these portraits and historical scenes were the work of an artist," Henley ventured to observe, looking at a strange head of Medusa.

"Yes," she answered, "the one you are looking at was done by Ah Ben."

He had been led to believe that Ah Ben was a living member of the household, who would shortly appear, but this now seemed impossible, for these extraordinary pictures were as old as the house itself. What did the girl mean? Had this Ah Ben done them all? Should he ask her and expose his ignorance? Paul thought he would venture upon a compromise.

"And are these pictures as old as they appear?"

"Quite," answered the girl. "As you can see for yourself, the house and all that is in it date from quite a remote time, and many of the portraits were painted before the house was ever begun."

That seemed to settle the question. Ah Ben was evidently a deceased ancestor; possibly a friend of the family in the distant past, and Henley concluded that he had misunderstood the girl in her former allusion to the man.

Dorothy had not taken off her hat, nor did she seem to have the slightest intention of doing so; meanwhile Paul's appetite, which had been temporarily lulled by his novel surroundings, was beginning to assert itself, and as there was no prospect of an attendant to conduct him to his room, he was about to ask where he might find a bowl of water to relieve himself of some of the stains of travel. Before he had finished the sentence, however, his attention was arrested by the sound of a distant footstep. He listened; it came nearer, and in a minute was descending the black staircase in the corner. Paul watched, and saw the figure of an old man as it turned an angle in the stairs. Then it stopped, and coughed lightly as if to announce its approach.

"Come," cried Dorothy, "it's only Mr. Henley, and I'm sure he'll be glad to see you."

The figure advanced, and when it had descended far enough to be in range with the fire and lamplight, Paul saw a most extraordinary person. The man, although very old, was tall and dignified in appearance, with deep-set, mysterious eyes, and flowing white moustache and hair. The top of his head was lightly bound in a turban of some flimsy material, and a loose robe of crimson silk hung from his shoulders, gathered together with a cord about the waist. As he advanced Henley observed that the bones of his cheeks were high and prominent, and the eyes buried so deep beneath their projecting brows and skull, that he was at a loss to account for the strange sense of power which he felt to be lodged in so small a space.

"This is Ah Ben, Mr. Henley, of whom I have spoken," said Dorothy, rising.

The old man extended his hand and bowed most courteously. He hoped that they had had a pleasant drive from the station, and then took his seat beside the fire.

Paul was dumfounded. Probably he was expected to know all about the man, and he had only just decided that he had been dead for a century. How could he so have misinterpreted what he had heard?

Ah Ben stretched his long bony fingers to the fire, and observed that the nights were beginning to grow quite cold.

"Yes," said Henley, "I had hardly expected to find the season so far advanced in your Southern home."

"Our altitude more than amends for our latitude," answered the old man; and then, taking a pair of massive tongs from the corner of the mantel, he stirred the balsam logs into a fierce blaze, starting a myriad of sparks in their flight up the chimney. Dorothy was looking above, and Paul, following the direction of her eyes, observed a model of Father Time reclining upon a shelf near the ceiling. The figure's scythe was broken; his limbs were in shackles, and his body covered with chains. It was an original conception, and Henley could not help asking if Time had really been checked in his onward march at Guir House.

"Ah!" said Dorothy, "that is a symbol of a great truth; but I am not surprised at your asking"; then, turning to the old man, added: "Mr. Henley has not yet been shown to his room, and I am sure he would like to see it. It is the west chamber."

"True," said Ah Ben, rising and taking a candle from the mantel, which he lighted with a firebrand; "if Mr. Henley will follow me, I shall take pleasure in pointing it out to him."

Paul followed the elder man up the black stairs, through devious passages, and past doors with pictured panels, until he began to wonder if he could ever find his way back again. At last they stopped before a rough door, hung with massive hinges stretching half way across it, discolored with rust, and looking as if they had not been moved in an age, and which creaked dismally as Ah Ben entered.

"This will be your room," he said, bowing courteously, and placing the candle upon the table near the chimney. He then reminded Henley that their evening meal would soon be ready. "If there is anything further which you will need, pray let me know," he added, and then retired.

"I should like my luggage," said Paul, having left it below, with the exception of a small satchel.

"It shall be sent to you at once," the old man answered, as he walked slowly away.

Left to himself, Henley looked around with curiosity. Every comfort had been provided, even to an arm-chair and writing-table by the fire; but the room, as well as its furnishing, was old and quaint, and rapidly going to decay. Everything he saw related to a past period of existence. The window was high, and deep set in the wall. There was a bench under it, upon which one was obliged to climb to obtain a view of the country, and Henley pulled himself up into the sill to look out.

The landscape presented an unbroken panorama of forest. No farming land was visible, and the distant mountains closed in the sky-line, and all bathed in the soft light of the moon, made a picture of extreme beauty and loneliness—a solid wilderness, shut in from the busy world without. There was a musty smell, as if the room had not been used in years, and he lifted the sash. The rich perfume of fir and balsam was wafted in, displacing the disagreeable odor.

The bed was a high four-poster, and there were steps for climbing into it. On examination, it was discovered to be built into the room with heavy timbers, and framed solidly with the house itself. A few faded rugs were scattered about the worm-eaten floor, and in every direction the wood-work was rough and unpainted, though massive enough for a fortress. Above the wash-stand was a strange picture, painted upon a fragment of coarse blanket, which had been stretched upon the wall. It depicted the setting sun, with red and gold rays, and a blue mountain in the distance. Around the entire scene, in a semicircle, was the word "Illusion," singularly wrought into the shafts of light, and undecipherable without the closest scrutiny. The figure of an old man in the foreground was contemplating the scene. It was a crude piece of work, but impressive. There was a large mahogany cabinet, mounted with brass; but its double doors were locked and its drawers immovable. Beside the bed was a worm-eaten door, and in idle curiosity Paul tried the handle. It opened easily, revealing a spacious closet, with hooks and shelves. Throwing the small satchel he had brought up with him upon the floor within, it struck something, but the closet was too dark for him to see what; so, taking the candle, he made an examination. In the farthest corner was a hand-rail, guarding a closed scuttle, in which was inserted a heavy iron ring. Henley took hold of the ring, and with some effort succeeded in opening the scuttle. Looking down, he found to his surprise that it communicated with a rough stairway leading below. He peered into the darkness, but could discern nothing save the steps, which seemed to go all the way to the cellar, and were just wide enough to admit of a human body. He then removed his belongings back into the room, shut down the scuttle, and closed the door. As there was no fastening, he wedged a chair between the knob and the floor, in such a manner that it could not be opened from within. He then threw himself upon the bed, wondering what would be the outcome of his unlawful enterprise, and while inhaling the tonic air of hill and forest, half wished he were well away from this uncanny house and its eccentric inmates. And yet, despite the mystery which enshrouded it, there was a charm, a fascination, he could not deny. It was the dream-like unreality of his surroundings—unreal, because different from all that he had ever known. Should he suddenly find himself a dozen miles removed, he felt certain that he would straightway return.

The musty smell had disappeared, and as the room was getting cold, Paul got up and closed the window. At the moment he had done so, there was a low knock at the door. He replied by a summons to enter, but there was no answer. The knock was repeated, and again Paul shouted, "Come in"; but, as before, there was no response. He now went to the door and opened it, and found a servant standing outside with his luggage.

"Why did you not come in?" Paul inquired.

But the man did not answer; he simply entered and placed the bags upon the floor. Henley now asked him another question, but the fellow did not even look at him, and left the room without saying a word. Suddenly Paul remembered that he had seen him before. It was the dumb man who had met them on their arrival. It was the only servant he had seen. Could it be possible that these people kept no other?

When Henley had completed his toilet, he blew out the candle and then groped his way down to the hall, where he found Miss Guir and Ah Ben awaiting him. The girl came forward to greet her guest, and to reveal her presence, the fire having died away and the hanging lamp affording but a dull, copperish glow, barely sufficient to indicate the furniture and outlines of the room.

Dorothy was radiant, but peculiarly so. She was unlike the girls to whom he was accustomed in the city. Moreover, her manner was more quiet, more earnest and dignified than theirs. She looked more charming than ever in a white gown, while her burnished hair was held in place by a tall Spanish comb, and decorated with a flower. To be sure, the details of her costume were only suggested in the vague, uncertain light, but her pose and manner were unusually impressive.

"I hope you will not think that all Virginians are as inhospitable as we appear to be, Mr. Henley," she exclaimed, with a graciousness that was quite bewitching.

"I'm sure," said Henley, "that I have never been treated with greater consideration by any one; my room is simply perfect!"

"In its way, yes; but its way is that of a century past. But what I was referring to in the matter of special negligence was the time we have kept you from food."

"Do you know," Paul replied, "that I have been so absorbed with the many strange things I have seen since my arrival that I have scarcely had time to think of food?"

"But I told you that you would be expected to have a good appetite."

"And I have. In fact, when I think of it, I am ravenous," he answered.

"Then follow me," she said, leading the way toward a heavily-curtained door upon the right. They passed into a narrow passage, and then, turning to the left, entered a softly-lighted room. Paul was amazed at the sight that met his eyes. A round table, set for two, loaded with flowers, cut glass, and silver, and lighted with wax candles grouped under a large central shade of yellow silk, with a deep fringe of the same material. The distant parts of the room were in comparative shadow forming a proper setting for the soft candlelight in the center. Evidently no one else was expected, and Dorothy, taking her seat upon one side of the cloth, requested Paul to sit opposite.

"And will not Ah Ben be with us?" inquired Henley, glancing around to see if the old man were not coming.

"I'm afraid not," replied Dorothy; "he rarely dines at this hour."

If Mr. Henley had been told of the reception awaiting him at Guir House before leaving New York, he would doubtless have considered it a hoax. As it was, he was astounded. The odd character of the house and its inmates had already given him much ground for thought, even amazement; but to suddenly find himself face to face, *tete-a-tete* with a bewitching girl, at a gorgeous dinner table, laid for them only, was a condition of things calculated to turn any ordinary man's head. Never for an instant had the girl given the slightest intimation of why he, or rather the original Henley, had been wanted, and every effort to gain a clew of his business was thwarted—sometimes, it seemed, intentionally. The table was deftly waited upon by the same dumb man, who was a man-of-all-work and marvelous capacity, but his orders were invariably given by signals. Paul wondered if he were mistaken; could it be another servant with the same affliction? But that seemed incredible.

Miss Guir's eloquent face, her wonderful hair and eyes, doubtless interfered with Paul in the full enjoyment of his meal. In fact, he was bewildered—dazed. He could neither account for the situation or the growing beauty of the girl. Was it the candle-light that had proved so becoming? But there was another matter that disturbed him, perhaps, quite as much as this. It was the fact that Dorothy would not eat. Scarcely a mouthful of food passed her lips, although the dishes were of the daintiest, and she barely tasted many which she recommended heartily to him. Was she ill? or was it not the usual hour for her evening meal? Manlike, Henley was distressed for anything not endowed with a hearty appetite, and after the long cool drive he was sure she ought to be hungry. When he ventured to allude to the fact, and to remark that neither she nor Ah Ben ate like country people, the girl only smiled and declared that they both ate quite enough for their health, although she would never undertake to judge for others. With this he had to be satisfied.

From time to time Paul's eyes would wander around the table; and from its dainty dishes and exquisite flowers return to their true lodestone, his hostess. In fact, the girl possessed a mesmeric charm for him, which had grown with marvelous rapidity since his arrival.

"It is all wonderfully beautiful!" he said, looking straight into Dorothy's eyes.

"I'm so glad you like it," she answered smiling, "but you're not eating like a very hungry man."

She was helping his plate to a salad of cresses, to which she was adding an extra spoonful of dressing.

"I think you will find this quite the correct thing," she added, pushing the plate toward him.

"Everything is much more than perfect," answered Paul; "in fact, I am not accustomed— —"

But he checked himself suddenly. How did he know what the real Henley was accustomed to? Possibly he was a millionaire, while he, Paul—was not.

Whate'er she was doing, in every pose, Miss Guir was a picture—a quaint, unusual picture, to be sure, but nevertheless a picture. In helping the fruit which was brought on after dinner, her white hands, ablaze with precious stones, shone to peculiar advantage; and when she poured out the coffee that followed, Paul wished for his kodak, for he had seen nowhere, save in old-fashioned engravings, just such a picture as she made. But it became Miss Guir's turn to be critical.

"Do you know what I think?" she said, looking him full in the face, and without a suspicion of embarrassment.

"About what?"

She bent toward him with her elbows on the table, her chin resting upon her clasped hands.

"I think that if you had a flower in your buttonhole—you wouldn't mind it now, would you, if I were to give you one?"

And then without either smile or apology, she took the chrysanthemum from her hair and tossed it over to Paul. There was something so odd, and yet so deeply earnest in the way the thing was done that Henley accepted the favor as he might have accepted a command from royalty than as a flirtatious banter from a girl. He placed the flower in his buttonhole without the faintest desire to respond with one of those frivolous speeches he would have used under most similar circumstances.

Before the meal was finished, Ah Ben entered the room and poured himself a cup of coffee, which he drank without sitting down. It was all that he took.

3

When Ah Ben had finished his coffee, the three retired to the great entrance hall, where the fire was burning brightly, and the hanging lamp lending its uncertain aid to the illumination of the curious old apartment. Ah Ben produced a couple of long-stemmed pipes, one of which he handed to Paul, with a great leather pouch of leaf tobacco which he showed his guest how to prepare for smoking. They seated themselves in the pew before the fire, Dorothy nearest the hearth, while Paul placed himself upon the lounge opposite.

A great stillness pervaded the house, and Mr. Henley could not help wondering again if there were not other members of the establishment. Dorothy was staring into the fire, her thoughts far away, while Ah Ben smoked his pipe in silence. "Perhaps they have theories about digestion," Paul reflected, while he pulled at his long Ti-ti stem, and watched the meditative couple before him. The firelight played upon Ah Ben's white moustache and swarthy features, and the colored handkerchief upon his head, and set the long thin fingers all of a tremble upon the pipe-stem, as if manipulating the stops of a flute. It danced over Dorothy's gown in a dazzling sheen of white, and flashed upon her jeweled hands in colored sparks of green and gold and purple and red, and lit up her face and hair with the soft warm tints of a Rubens. Such a picture did the twain combine to make; they looked indeed as if they might have stepped from the canvas of some old master and come for a brief season to taste the joys of flesh and blood and life.

The outer regions of the hall were in darkness, the ancient lamp barely revealing the oddities of brush, chisel, and structure, that combined to make the most remarkable living-room that Henley had ever seen. The decaying portraits, the singular carvings and peculiar furniture, now only revealed themselves by suggestion in the faint illumination of the lamp and uncertain flicker of the fire.

But what were these people, Dorothy and Ah Ben, to each other? It was out of the question that they could be husband and wife—it seemed equally so that they could be father and daughter. Paul searched the faces of each for traces of similiarity, but there were none. Their manner to each other, the girl's mode of addressing the man, all indicated the absence of kinship. Yes, Henley felt quite certain that Ah Ben and Dorothy Guir were neither related nor connected, and that they were never likely to become so.

From time to time the old man would arise to mend the fire, and a quiet conversation upon indifferent topics ensued, Dorothy uttering a few words occasionally, in a dreamy voice, with her head propped upon a cushion in the corner. At last she failed to answer when spoken to; evidently she had fallen asleep.

"My daughter, you need rest," said Ah Ben gently, and at the same moment a clock upon the stairs began striking eleven.

Dorothy opened her eyes and looked around.

"I must have fallen asleep!" she exclaimed quite naively.

She bade them each "Good night," and then started up the uncanny stairs. Near the top she paused in the darkness, and looking over the balustrade into the hall below, seemed to be waiting. Perhaps she was not so completely in the shadow as she imagined, and perhaps Paul did not see aright, but through the gloom he thought he caught the flash of a diamond as it moved toward her lips and away again. If tempted to return the salute, his better judgment prevailed, and while holding the stem of his pipe in his right hand, pressed the tobacco firmly into the bowl with his left. A troublesome thought presented itself. Could this girl have entered into any kind of entanglement with his namesake which would have demanded a tenderer attitude than he had assumed toward her? Had he neglected opportunities and failed to avail himself of privileges which he had unknowingly inherited? For an instant the thought disturbed Mr. Henley's equilibrium, but a moment's reflection convinced him that the idea was not worth considering. Whatever it was he had seen upon the stairs he knew was not intended for his eyes, even if it had been meant for himself.

"Shall we smoke another pipe?" said Ah Ben. "I'm something of an owl myself, and shall sit here for quite a while before retiring."

Paul was glad of the opportunity, and accepted with alacrity. He hoped in the quiet of a midnight conversation to discover something about this peculiar man and his home. Perhaps he should also learn something of the girl, her strange life, and the Guirs.

"We may not be so comfortable as we would be in our beds," continued the elder man, "but there is a certain comfort in discomfort which ought not to be undervalued. Sleep, to be enjoyed, should be discouraged rather than courted."

"Yes," answered Paul, "I believe Shakespeare has told us something about it in his famous soliloquy on that subject."

"True," replied Ah Ben, "and I suppose there is no one living who has not felt the delusion of comfort. Like many other material blessings, it is to be had only in pills."

Ah Ben had stretched his legs out toward the hearth, and while passing his hand across his withered cheek, had closed his eyes in reverie. The dim and uncertain shadows made the room seem like some vast cavern, whose walls were mythical and whose recesses unexplored. The lamp had expired to a single spark, and there was nothing to reveal their presence to each other except the red glow from the embers.

"No," said the man, continuing to speak with his eyes still closed, "luxury is not necessary to a man's happiness, although he has persuaded himself that it is so."

"Perhaps not," Paul admitted, "although I contend that a certain amount of comfort is."

"By no means. There was never a greater fallacy, although I am free to admit that under certain conditions it may conduce to that end. But tell me, have you never seen one happy amid the greatest physical privations?"

"Not absolutely."

"No, not absolutely; the absolute does not belong to the finite. I refer to what most men would consider happiness."

"Oh, if you're talking about saints, they're outside my experience."

A faint smile played over Ah Ben's face as he answered:

"Saints, my dear sir, are no more to me than to you. Have you ever seen a prize fight?"

"Oh, yes; several."

"Do you not believe that the winner of a prize fight, even when covered with bruises, and suffering in every bone of his body, is happier at the moment of victory than he was the previous morning while lying comfortably in his bed?"

"I dare say; but now you're speaking of— "

"Happiness," suggested Ah Ben, "and if you will pardon me for saying so—for possibly I may have thought more upon this subject than you have—I can tell you the one essential which lies at the root of all happiness, without which it can never be acquired, but with which it is certain to follow."

"And what is that?" inquired Paul, with interest.

"*Power*" said Ah Ben, with an assurance that left no doubt of the conviction of the speaker.

"I suppose that is a kind of stepping-stone to contentment," answered Paul, reflectively.

"Precisely; for no man who lacks the power to accomplish his desires can know contentment. But contentment is transitory, and rests upon power. Power alone is the cornerstone of happiness."

"Do you really believe that?" Paul inquired, half incredulously.

"I know it. With me it is not a matter of speculation; it is a matter of knowledge."

"Then let me ask you why it is that the greatest power in the world, which is undoubtedly money, so often fails of this end?"

Ah Ben refilled his pipe, then raked a coal out of the fire with the bowl and pressed it firmly down upon the tobacco, and then said, reflectively:

"You are mistaken. Money does confer happiness to the full limit of its power, but this limit is quickly reached—first, because man's ambitions and desires grow faster than his wealth, or reach out into channels that wealth can never compass, or, and principally, because wealth is an impersonal power and not a direct one. Give the earth to a single man, and it would never enable him to change his appearance or alter one of his mental characteristics, nor to do one single thing he could not have accomplished before—it giving him the power to make others do his will; and so long as his will is not beyond the power of others to do, he is to that extent happy. But to be really happy, a man must have *personal power*. Wealth is not power. Power is lodged in the individuality."

"I don't know whether I quite understand you," said Paul.

Ah Ben looked at him searchingly with his luminous, deep-set eyes.

"Can gold restore an idiot's mind," he inquired, "or a cripple the use of his limbs? Would a mountain of gold add one iota to the power of your soul? And yet it is gold that men have labored for since the earth was made. Could they once understand its real limitations? What a different planet we should have!"

"That is all very well," answered Henley; "but this personal power of which you speak is born in a man, and is not to be acquired by anything he can do; whereas, the battle for wealth can be fought in a field open to all."

"There again I must beg to differ from you," said Ah Ben. "There is a law for the acquirement of this soul-power which is as fixed and certain as the law of gravitation; and when a man has once gained it, he has no more use for worldly wealth than he has for the drainings of a sewer."

"Do you mean to say that by a course of life— "

"I do, and it is this: *Self-control is the law of psychic power*."

"Then, according to your theory, the better mastery a man has over himself, the more he can accomplish and the greater his happiness?"

"I go still further," the old man continued. "I claim that *self-control is the only source of happiness, and that he who can control his body—and by this I mean his eyes, his nerves, his tongue, his appetites and passions—can control other men; but he who is master of his mind, his thoughts, his desires, his emotions, has the world in a sling. Such a man is all powerful;*

there is nothing he can not accomplish; there is no force that can stand against him."

The fire had died out, save for a few glowing embers, but Ah Ben's singular face seemed to draw unto itself what light there was, and to hold Henley's eyes in a kind of mesmeric fascination. He had put off going to bed for the sole purpose of gaining some knowledge of the house and its inmates; and yet now, with apparently nothing to hinder his investigations, he felt an unaccountable diffidence about making the inquiries. An impression that the man was a mind-reader had doubtless increased this embarrassment, and yet he had had no evidence of this kind, nor anything to indicate such a fact beyond the keen, penetrating power of those marvelous eyes. Paul felt that there was a mental chasm, deep and wide and impassable, that yawned between him and the strange individual before him. Such stupendous power of will as lodged within that brain could sport with the forces of nature, suspend or reverse the action of law, disintegrate matter, or create it. At least such was the impression which Mr. Henley had received.

It was past midnight before a movement was made for bed, and when Ah Ben brought a lighted candle, inquiring if everything in the bedchamber had been satisfactory, Paul was about to reply in the affirmative, when he suddenly remembered the staircase in the closet.

"I was about to forget," he said, "but would you mind explaining the object of a very peculiar staircase I discovered in the closet of my room?"

"This house is old," Ah Ben replied simply. "It was built when the State was a colony and full of Indians. The stairway communicating with the lower floor was doubtless intended as a means of escape. I had not thought of this annoying you, but can readily see how it might. You shall be removed to another room at once."

"*Removed*?" exclaimed Paul. "My dear sir, I had no intention of making such a suggestion. The most I thought of asking for was a bolt for the door, or scuttle; but since your explanation I do not wish either."

They bade each other good night, and Paul undertook to find his room alone, declining Ah Ben's offer to accompany him. But the house was full of strange passages and unexpected stairways, making the task more difficult than he had expected. After wandering about he found himself stopped by a dead wall, at least so it had looked, but suddenly directly before him stood Ah Ben.

"I thought you might need my assistance," he said quietly; and then without appearing to notice Henley's astonishment, led the way to his room.

When Paul found himself alone, he became conscious of a growing curiosity concerning the stairs in the closet. He opened the door and looked in, and then quietly lifted the scuttle by the ring. He peered down into the darkness, but, as the stairs were winding, could discern nothing for more than a half dozen steps below. He listened, but the house was perfectly quiet, Ah Ben's retreating footsteps having died upon the air. Somehow he half doubted the story which the old man had told him about the original intention of the stairway as a means of escape. It seemed improbable, and dated back to such a remote period that he could not help feeling distrustful. Candle in hand, he commenced to descend, looking carefully where he placed his feet. As everywhere else, the woodwork was worm-eaten, and the timbers set up a dismal creaking under the weight of his body, but he had undertaken to investigate the meaning of this architectural eccentricity, and would not now turn back. On he crept, noiselessly as possible, adown the twisting stairs, carefully looking ahead for pitfalls and unsuspected developments. Once he paused, thinking he heard the distant tread of a foot, but the sound died away, and he resumed his course. Some of the steps were so broken and rotten that extreme caution was necessary to avoid falling. At last he reached the ground, and found himself at the bottom of a square well, around the four walls of which the stairs had been built. He was facing a massive door, which occupied one of the sides of the well. Paul tried the lock, but it was so old and rust-eaten that it refused to move. There was no other outlet, and the place was narrow and damp. He looked wistfully at the solitary door, feeling a vague suspicion that it barred the entrance to a mystery, and resolved to return at some future time, when not so harassed with sleepiness and the fatigues of travel, and make another effort to open it. Paul looked above, and as he did so a gust of air swept down the narrow opening and blew out his light; at the same instant he heard the fall of the scuttle and realized that he was shut in.

"Trapped! and by my own cursed curiosity," he muttered, as he commenced groping his way up in the darkness. But it was not so easy as he had supposed. Twice he slipped his foot into a rotten hole, and once the stairs trembled so violently that he thought they were about to fall. Nevertheless he reached the top, as he realized when his head came in contact with the trap-door, upon the other side of which he pictured Ah Ben standing with an amused smile. Henley placed his shoulder against the door, and to his amazement found that it opened quite easily. He then procured a light, and having satisfied himself that there had never been the slightest intention to entrap him, the door having simply fallen, he went hurriedly to bed.

4

The breakfast room was a charming little corner reclaimed from a dingy cell, where in by-gone days guns and ammunition had been stored, but the peace-loving inhabitants of later times had rendered these no longer necessary. It was now the most modern room Paul had seen since his arrival at this great unconventional homestead, looking quite as if it had been tacked on by mistake to the dismal old mansion.

Upon entering, he found Miss Guir sitting alone at the table. She was attired in a charming costume, and looked as fresh as the flowers before her. She greeted him with a smile, and asked how he had slept.

"Perfectly!" he answered, seating himself by her side, where he looked out of a low French window opening upon a garden with boxwood borders and a few belated blossoms.

"But do you know," he continued, "the most extraordinary thing happened."

He went on to tell of his experience in the closet, thinking it best to take the *bull by the horns* and see if anything in Dorothy's expression would lead him to suspect foul play. She listened to his story with interest, and, as Paul thought, a slight display of anxiety, but nothing more. When he had finished, she simply advised him not to go down those stairs any more, as they were rotten and dangerous. This was all. Nevertheless Henley felt sure that the girl knew what lay upon the other side of the door at the bottom. They chatted along quite pleasantly, Paul endeavoring to lead the conversation into some instructive channel, but without success.

"I thought perhaps I should have met some of your people at breakfast," he said, while sipping his coffee.

Dorothy stopped with a piece of toast half way to her lips.

"*My people*!" she exclaimed.

"Yes," said Paul, unmindful of the impression he had made.

"Really, Mr. Henley, what are you talking about?"

"The Guirs!" said Paul, still unheedful.

Suddenly he looked up, and the expression on the girl's face startled him.

"Are you ill?" he cried. "Is there anything I can do for you?"

"No, no," she gasped. "It is nothing. I am nervous. I am always nervous in the morning, and you gave me quite a turn. There now, I shall feel better directly."

If Paul was astonished before, he was dumfounded now. He could not imagine how anything he had said could produce such an effect, but he watched the return of color to the girl's face with satisfaction. Presently she looked up at him with a smile and said:

"It is all right now, but you must excuse me for a minute. I shall be back immediately."

She got up and left the room, leaving Paul alone. His appetite had quite departed, so he turned his chair around and looked out of the window at the boxwood bushes and the trees beyond. Not a human figure was in sight, nor was there a sound to indicate that there were living creatures about the premises. Where was the family? Surely such a large house could not be occupied solely by the few individuals he had already met. If there were other members, where had they kept themselves? He would have given the world to have asked a few straightforward questions, but there seemed no opportunity to do so. Where was Ah Ben? Even he had not shown his face at the breakfast table. A painful sense of mystery was growing more oppressive each hour, which the bright morning sunlight had not dispelled, as he had hoped it would. If this feeling had confined itself to Ah Ben and the house, Paul thought he might have shaken off the gloom while in the company of the girl, but even she was subject to such extraordinary flights of eccentricity, such sudden fits of nervous depression, that he felt she was not surely to be depended on as a solace to his troubled soul. While he was meditating, the door opened, and Dorothy returned. She was full of smiles; and the color had come back to her cheeks.

"I can't imagine how I could have given you such a turn," said Paul apologetically, as he resumed his place at the table.

"It was altogether my fault," she answered. Then looking at him very earnestly, added:

"I hope, Mr. Henley, that you may never become an outcast, as I am. I hope *your people* will never disown you. But let us talk of something else."

As upon the previous evening, she was solicitous about his food, that it should be of the best, and that he should enjoy it, although apparently indifferent about her own.

"Of course, you will find us quite different from other people, Mr. Henley," she continued, sipping her coffee (she never seemed to drink or eat anything heartily); "our ideas and manner of living being quite at variance with theirs."

"Yes," Paul replied, as if he understood it perfectly. She was toying with her cup as though not knowing exactly how to continue. Presently she looked up at him appealingly, possessed of a sudden idea, and added:

"And what do you think about the brain?"

Paul was astonished at the irrelevancy of the question.

"I think it is in the head," he answered, smiling, in the hope of averting a difficulty. "That is, I think it ought to be there," he added in a minute, "although it is doubtless missing in some cases. Still, there can be but little dissent from the general opinion that the skull is the proper place for it."

She looked puzzled, and Paul began to wonder if he had offended her, but in another moment she relaxed into a smile.

"I'm sure you don't think anything of the kind," she answered, "for if you do, you're not up to date. The latest investigations have shown that brain matter is distributed throughout the body. No, I'm not joking. We all think more or less with our hands and feet."

"I've not the slightest doubt of it," Paul answered, applying himself to his food; "and even if I had," he continued, "I should never dispute anything you told me." And then, looking her full in the face, he added: "Do you know, Miss Guir, that you have exerted a most remarkable influence over me? It might not be polite to say that it is inexplicable; but when I recall the fact that no girl ever before, in so short a time— "

He paused for a word, but before he could discover one that was satisfactory, she said:

"Do you mean to say that you have formed a liking for me already?"

"It is hardly the word. I have been fascinated from the moment I first saw you."

"I'm so glad," she answered, without the slightest appearance of coquetry, and as simply and naturally as though she were talking about the weather. Paul was puzzled. He could not understand her, and not knowing how to proceed, an awkward silence followed. Presently she leaned her head upon her hand, her elbow resting on the table, and with a languid yet interested scrutiny of his face, said:

"You doubtless know the world, its people and ways, far better than I, and perhaps you wouldn't mind helping me with my book."

"Indeed! You are writing a book, then?"

"No, but I should like to do so."

"And may I ask what it is about?"

"It's about myself and Ah Ben, and the awful predicament into which we have fallen."

"I should like greatly to help you," said Paul, thinking the subject might lead to a clearer insight of the situation; "but even were I competent to do so, which I doubt, I can not see how any little worldly knowledge I might possess could possibly be of service in a description of your own life."

"It is only that I should like to present our story in attractive form—one which would be read by worldly people."

"A laudable ambition. But what is the predicament you speak of?"

"The predicament is more directly my own; the situation, Ah Ben's."

"Perhaps if you will explain them, I might aid you."

"You might indeed," she answered seriously, rising from the table; "but it would be premature. Let us go into the garden."

She led the way through the back of the house out into the old-fashioned yard, where boxwood bushes and chrysanthemums, together with other autumnal flowers, adorned the beds. They walked down a straight path and seated themselves upon a rustic bench in full view of the edifice. Paul lighted a cigarette and watched the strange old building before him, while Dorothy was content to sit and look at him, as though he were some new variety of man just landed from the planet Mars. Presently she arose and wandered down the path in search of a few choice blossoms, leaving Paul alone, who watched her until she disappeared among the shrubbery.

Sitting quietly smoking his cigarette, Mr. Henley became absorbed in a critical study of the quaint old pile which had so suddenly risen to abnormal interest in his eyes. A part of the structure was falling rapidly to decay, while other portions were so deeply embedded in ivy and other creeping things that it was impossible to discover their actual state of preservation. The windows were small and far apart, and Paul recognized his own by its bearing upon a certain tree which he had noticed while looking out upon the previous night. Following down the line of the wall, he was surprised to find a large space which was not pierced by either door or window, and naturally began to wonder what manner of apartment lay upon the opposite side, where neither light nor air were admitted. The wall, to be sure, was covered with Virginia creeper, which had made its way to the roof, but it was evident that it concealed no opening. Then his thoughts wandered back to the mysterious well, and he began to wonder if the closed door at the bottom connected with the unaccounted-for space behind this wall. His curiosity grew as he brooded upon this possibility—a possibility which he now conceded to be a certainty as he marked the configuration of the building. The blank wall was beneath his bedroom. The well descended directly into it, or upon one side of it, and communicated with it through the door mentioned. There was nothing to be learned by inquiry, and Henley determined to make another effort to force open the door. His resolution was not entirely the result of curiosity, for he had taken such a sudden and strong liking for the girl that he disliked the thought of leaving her; and yet the riddle of her environment was such that he conceived it to be no more than a proper regard for his own safety to take such a precaution while visiting her. Having reached this determination, he cast about for the means of executing it. He thought he should require a hammer and a cold chisel, but where such were to be found he could not conceive. Moreover, even were they in his possession, it was impossible to see exactly how he could make use of them without arousing the household. He thought of various devices, such as a muffled hammer, or a crowbar to wrench the door from its hinges, but these were discarded in turn as impracticable, from the fact that they were unobtainable. He looked about him among the shrubbery, but there was nothing to aid him; and, indeed, how could he expect to find tools where there were no servants to use them? He got up and walked down the path, absorbed in reverie, and although unable to devise any immediate plan to accomplish the task, his resolution became more fixed as he dwelt upon it. He would risk all things in opening that door, and was impatient for an opportunity to renew the effort. Then the girl's voice came floating through the air in a plaintive melody, and Henley was recalled to his surroundings. In another minute she had joined him.

"I was afraid you would be lonely without me," she said, "and so I returned as soon as I had carried the flowers to the house."

"I am so glad," he replied, with a look of unmistakable pleasure. "Do you know, this is the most romantic place I have ever seen in all my life, and you are certainly the most romantic girl."

"Am I?" she answered sadly, and without a glimmering suspicion of a smile.

They walked slowly down the path until reaching a decrepit old gate, where they stopped.

"This is the end of the garden," she said. "Shall we go into the woods for a walk?"

"Dorothy!" Paul began, "pardon me for calling you by your name, but do you know I feel as if any prefix in your case would be irritating, from the fact that you strike me as a girl who is utterly above and beyond such idle conventionalities. One would almost as soon think of saying Miss to a goddess."

"And may I call you Paul? You will not think me forward if I should do so?" she asked, looking up at him.

"I will think myself more honored than any poor language of mine could describe," he answered.

"You know I would not want to call you Paul," she added, "unless I believed in you—unless I thought you were true and honorable in all things."

Paul winced. Was he not deceiving the girl at that very minute? What could he say?

"Dorothy," he answered, after a moment's hesitation, "I am not true, nor honorable neither. Perhaps you had better not call me Paul. I do not deserve it."

She was looking him straight in the face, with her hand upon the gate. He felt the keen, searching quality of her eyes, but was able now to return the look.

"We sometimes judge ourselves harshly," she continued. "I have myself been often led by an idle temptation into what at first appeared but a trifling wrong, but which looked far more serious later. Had I acted with the greater knowledge, I had committed the greater fault."

What was she saying? Was she not describing his own position?

"Therefore, when I say Paul," she added, "I do it because I like you, and because I believe in you, and not because I think you perfect."

She lifted the rickety old gate with care, and he closed it after them; then they walked out over the dank leaves, through the brilliant coloring of the forest. The day was soft and tempting, while a mellow haze filled the air.

"I am going to show you the prettiest spot in all the world," said Dorothy, "a place where I often go and sit alone."

They walked side by side, there being no longer any path, or, if there had been one, it was now covered, and the sunlight, filtering through the tree-tops, fell in brilliant patches upon the gaudy carpet beneath their feet. They had walked a mile, when Paul heard the murmur of distant water, and saw that they were heading for a rocky gorge, through which a small stream forced its way in a jumble of tiny cataracts and pools. It was an ideal spot, shut in from all the world beyond. The restful air, barely stirring the tree-tops, and the water, as it went dripping from stone to stone, made just enough sound to intimate that the life principle of a drowsy world was existent. They seated themselves upon a rocky ledge, and Dorothy became absorbed in reverie; while Paul, from a slightly lower point, gazed up at the trees, the sky, and the girl, with mute infatuation.

"You lead such an ideal life here," he said, after some minutes of silence, "that I should imagine the outer world would seem harsh and cold by contrast."

"But I have never seen what you call the outer world," she answered, with a touch of melancholy in her voice.

"Do you mean to say that you have lived here always?"

"Yes, and always shall, unless some one helps me away."

"I don't think I quite understand," he replied, "who could help you away, if your own people would not. Pardon the allusion, but I do not grasp the situation."

"I could never go with any of the Guirs," she answered, with a shudder, "for I am quite as much afraid of them as they are of me."

Paul was again silent. He was meditating whether it were best to ask frankly what she meant, and risk the girl's displeasure, as well as his own identity, or to take another course. Presently he said:

"Dorothy, I would not pry into the secrets of your soul for the world, and am sure you will believe in my honesty in declaring that there is no one whom I would more gladly serve than yourself. I think you must know this."

An eager glance for a moment dispelled the melancholy of her face, and then the old look returned with added force, as she answered:

"Yes, Paul, I believe what you say, and admit that you, of all men, could be of service; and yet you have no conception of the sacrifice you would entail upon yourself by the service you would render. Could I profit myself at the cost of your eternal sorrow? You do not know, and alas! I cannot explain; but the boon of my liberty would, I fear, only be purchased at the price of yours. I had not thought I should be so perplexed!"

He had not found the slightest relief from the embarrassing ignorance that enshrouded him. The girl's utter lack of coquetry, and her depth of feeling, made his position even more complex than it might otherwise have been.

"As you must know, I am talking in the dark," he continued after a minute, "but this much I will venture to assert, that no act of mine could be a sacrifice which would put my life in closer touch with yours; for although it was only yesterday that we met for the first time, I love you; and I loved you, Dorothy, from the instant I first caught sight of you at the station. I do not pretend to explain this, but have felt an overpowering passion from that moment."

"And you will not think me unmaidenly, Paul, if I say the same to you?"

She made no effort to conceal her feelings, and they sat murmuring sweet things into each other's ears until a green bird came fluttering through the air, and lighting upon a bough just above their heads, screamed:

"Dorothy! Dorothy!"

It was a parrot, and there was something so uncanny in its sudden appearance that Paul started:

"He seems to be your chaperone!" he observed.

"He is my mascot!" cried Dorothy. "If it were not for his company, I fear I should go mad. I am so lonely, Paul, you can not understand it."

"Have you no neighbors?" he inquired.

"None within miles; and we live such a strange isolated life that people are afraid of us."

Paul thought of the stage driver, and his look of horror on hearing where he was going.

"I can't understand why people should be afraid of you simply because you live alone," he said. "For my part, I think your life here is most interesting. But you have not told me how I can help you."

"Nor can I yet," she answered. "There is a way, of course, but I can not consent to so great a sacrifice from you; at least, not at present."

"And would it compel me to leave you?"

"No; it would compel you to be with me always."

"And have you so little faith in me as to call that a sacrifice? I did flatter myself that you believed what I told you just now."

"But, Paul, you do not know me. Wait until you do. Then, perhaps, you will change your mind."

She spoke with emphasis and a strange depth of feeling, and he wondered what she meant.

"I could never change, Dorothy," he replied with fervor, "unless you wished it; but if you did, do you know I believe it would not be in your power to reverse the bewildering spell you have wrought, and make me hate you, for never before have I felt anything approaching this strange sudden infatuation. But do not keep me in suspense; tell me, I pray, what is this mystery in your life which you think would change my feelings toward you?"

"I belong nowhere. I have no friend in all the wide world," she answered bitterly.

"You have forgotten Ah Ben," suggested Paul. She did not answer, but continued stroking the parrot which had lighted upon her shoulder, demanding her caresses with numerous mutterings.

"Modesty prevents my reminding you of my humble aspirations to your friendship," added Paul, nestling closer to her side. Suddenly she looked up at him with an intense penetrating gaze, while she squeezed the parrot until it screamed.

"Do you think you could show your friendship and stick to me through a terrible ordeal?" she asked earnestly.

"I'm sure of it," he answered. "My love is not so thin-skinned as to shrink from any test. Only try me!"

"Then get me away from this place," she cried, "far, *far* away from it. But, mind, it will not be so easy as you think."

"Are you held against your will?" demanded Paul.

"No, *no*! You can not understand it. But I could not go alone. I will explain it to you some time, but not now. There is no hurry."

"Is Ah Ben anxious to keep you?" inquired Henley.

"On the contrary, he wishes me to go. You can not understand me, as I am quite different from other girls. Only take my word for what I tell you; and when the time comes, you will not desert me, will you?"

There was something wildly entreating in her manner and the tones of her voice, and a pathos which went to Henley's heart. What it all was about he could no more imagine than he could account for any of the mysteries at Guir House; but he was determined to stand by Dorothy, come what might.

Suddenly the girl had become quiet, rapt in some new thought. In another minute she placed her hand lightly upon Paul's shoulder, and said:

"Remember, you have promised!"

"I have promised," answered Paul. "Is there anything more?"

"Yes," said Dorothy.

She paused for a minute, as if what she were about to say was a great effort.

"Well," he continued, "after I have got you safely away—which, by the by, does not seem such a difficult task, as no one opposes your going—but, after we have escaped together, what further am I to do?"

"Naturally, I feel great delicacy in what I am about to say," said Dorothy; "but since you have told me that you love me, it does not seem so hard, although you do not know who or what I am—but, to be candid and frank with you, dear Paul, after you have gotten me away—why, you must marry me!"

Paul snatched her up in his arms.

"My darling!" he said, "you are making me the proudest man on earth!"

"Do not speak too soon," said Dorothy, releasing herself from his grasp. "Remember I have told you frankly that you do not know me. Perhaps I am driving a hard bargain with you!"

For a moment Paul became serious.

"Tell me, Dorothy," he asked, in an altered tone, "have you, or Ah Ben, or any member of your mysterious household or family, any crimes to answer for? Is there any good reason why I, as an honest man, should object to taking you for my wife?"

She turned scarlet as she answered:

"Never! There is no such reason. There is nothing dishonorable, I swear to you—nothing which could implicate you in any way with wrong-doing. No, Paul; my secret is different from that. You could never guess it, nor could I ever compromise you with crime."

Her manner was sincere, and carried conviction to the hearer of the truth of what she said.

"It is time we were going to the house," she added, rising, with the parrot still upon her shoulder; and side by side they retraced their steps along the woodland way homeward.

5

Although Mr. Henley had no doubt of the truth of Miss Guir's assertion, the mystery of her life was as real and deeply impressive as ever. Perhaps it was even more so, as seeming more subtle and far-reaching than crime itself, if such a thing were possible. Paul was determined to investigate the secret of the closet stairs; for while Ah Ben's explanation was plausible to a degree, the blank wall and heavy door at the bottom filled him with an uncanny fascination, which grew as he pondered upon them. Exactly what course to pursue he had not decided, but awaited an opportunity to continue his efforts in earnest. There were two serious difficulties to contend with; one was the want of tools, the other the necessity of prosecuting his work in silence.

As upon the previous evening, Dorothy and Mr. Henley dined alone, although Ah Ben, appearing just before they had finished, partook of a little dry lettuce and a small cup of coffee. Dorothy, as usual, ate most sparingly, "scarcely enough," as Paul remarked, "to keep the parrot alive."

After dinner they went together into the great hall, where Ah Ben prepared a pipe apiece for himself and his guest.

The logs were piled high upon the hearth, and the cheery blaze lit up the old pictures with a shimmering lustre, reducing the lamp to a mere spectral ornament. It was the flickering firelight that made the men and women on the walls nod at each other, as perhaps they had done in life.

They seated themselves in the spacious old leather-covered pew; Ah Ben and Dorothy upon one side, while Paul sat opposite. The men were soon engaged with their pipes, while Miss Guir had settled herself upon a pile of cushions in the corner nearest the chimney.

"You have been absent from home to-day, I believe," said Henley to the old man, by way of opening the conversation, and with the hope of eliciting an answer which would throw some light upon his habits.

"Yes," Ah Ben replied, blowing a volume of smoke from under his long, white moustache; "I seldom pass the entire day in this house. There are few things that give me more pleasure than roaming alone through the forest. One seems to come in closer touch with first principles. Nature, Mr. Henley, must be courted to be comprehended."

"I suppose so," answered Paul, not knowing what else to say, and wondering at the man's odd method of passing the time.

A long silence followed after this, only interrupted at intervals by guttural mutterings from the parrot, which seemed to be lodged somewhere in the upper regions of the obscure stairway. When the clock struck eleven, the bird shrieked out, as upon the previous night.

"Dorothy! Dorothy! it is bed time!"

Miss Guir arose, and saying "Good night," left Ah Ben and Mr. Henley to themselves.

"I am afraid I have been very stupid," said the old man, apologetically; "indeed, I must have fallen asleep, as it is my habit to take a nap in the early evening, after which I am more wide awake than at any other hour."

"Not at all," answered Paul, "I have been enjoying my pipe, and as Miss Guir seemed disposed to be quiet, think I must have been nodding myself."

"Do you feel disposed to join me in another pipe and a midnight talk," inquired the host, "or are you inclined for bed?"

Paul was not sleepy, and nothing could have suited him better than to sit over the fire, listening to this strange man, and so he again accepted eagerly. Ah Ben seemed pleased, declaring it was a great treat to have a friend who was as much of an owl as he himself was. And so he added fresh fuel to the dying embers, settled himself in his cosy corner by the fire, while Paul sat opposite.

"Every man must live his own life," resumed Ah Ben; "but with my temper, the better half would be blotted out, were I deprived of this quiet time for thought and reflection."

"I quite agree with you," replied Paul, "and yet the wisdom of the world is opposed to late hours,"

"The wisdom of the world is based upon the experience of the *worldly prosperous*; and what is worldly prosperity but the accumulation of dollars? To be prosperous is one thing; to be happy, quite another."

"I see you are coming back to our old argument. I am sure I could never school myself to the cheerful disregard for money which you seem to have. For my part, I could not do without it, although, to be sure, I sometimes manage on very little."

"Again the wisdom of the world!" exclaimed Ah Ben, "and what has it done for us?"

"It has taught us to be very comfortable in this latter part of the nineteenth century," Paul replied.

"Has it?" cried the old man, his eyes fixed full upon Henley's face. "I admit," he continued, "that it has taught us to rely upon luxuries that eat out the life while pampering the body. It has taught us to depend upon the poison that paralyzes the will, and that personal power we were speaking of. It has done much for man, I grant you, but its efforts have been mainly directed to his destruction."

"No man can be happy without health," answered Paul, "and surely you will admit that the discoveries of the last few decades have done much to improve his physical condition."

He was nestling back into the corner of his lounge, where the shadow of the mantelpiece screened his face, and enabled him to look directly into Ah Ben's eyes, now fixed upon him with strange intensity. There was a power behind those eyes that was wont to impress the beholder with a species of interest which he felt might be developed into awe; and yet they were neither large nor handsome, as eyes are generally counted. Deep set, mounted with withered lids and shaggy brows, their power was due to the manifestation of a spiritual force, a Titanic will, that made itself felt, independent of material envelopment. It was the soul looking through the narrow window of mortality.

"Health?" said Ah Ben, repeating Henley's last idea interrogatively, and yet scarcely above a whisper.

"Yes, health," answered Paul. "I maintain that the old maxim of 'early to bed' says something on that score, as well as on that of wealth."

"True, but you said that a man must needs be healthy to be happy."

"That's it, and I maintain that it's a pretty good assertion."

"There again we must differ. Happiness should be independent of bodily conditions, whether those conditions mean outward luxury or inward ease. I must again refer you to the prize-fighter. But if you will pardon me, I think you have put the cart before the horse; for once having granted that personal power, happiness must ensue, and your health as a necessity follow. First cultivate this occult force, and we need submit to no physical laws; for inasmuch as the higher controls the lower, we are masters of our own bodies."

"That is a pretty good prescription for those who are able to follow it, but for my humble attainments I'd rather depend on physic and a virtuous life."

"Quite so," answered Ah Ben, thoughtfully, "but, speaking frankly, this limitation of your powers to the chemical action of your body only shows the narrowness of your scientific training. Had men been taught the power of the will as the underlying principle of every effect, one drug would have proved quite as efficacious as another, and bread pills would have met the requirements of the world."

"But in the state of imbecility in which we happen to find ourselves," added Paul, "I should think that a judicious application of the world's wisdom would be better than trifling with theories one does not comprehend."

"As I said just now," observed Ah Ben, "I have no desire to force my private views upon another, but I must distinctly object to the word 'theory,' as associated with my positive knowledge on this subject. Every man must do as he thinks right, and as suits him best; but, for my part, I have disregarded all the physical laws of health during an unusually long life."

Paul straightened himself up, and looked at his host in the hope of a further explanation.

"I don't think I quite understand you!"

"Yes," said Ah Ben, repeating the sentence slowly and emphasizing the words, "*I disregard all laws usually considered essential to living at all*!"

Henley was silent for a minute in a vain effort to decide whether or not he were speaking seriously. He could not help remembering his abstinence from food, but at the time had not doubted the man had eaten between meals.

"Then you certainly ought to know all about it," he continued, relaxing into his former position, but quite unsettled as to Ah Ben's intention.

"You must admit that I have had sufficient time to be an authority unto myself, if not to others," added the old man. And then as he pressed the ashes down into the bowl of his pipe with his long emaciated fingers, and watched the little threads of smoke as they came curling out from under his thick moustache, Paul could only admit that the gravity of his bearing was inconsistent with a humorous interpretation of his words.

"You interest me greatly," resumed Henley, after scrutinizing the singular face before him for several minutes, in a kind of mesmeric fascination, "and I should like to ask what you mean by the cultivation of this occult power of which you spoke?"

"It is only to be acquired by the supremest quality of self-control, as I told you yesterday," answered Ah Ben; "but when once gained, no man would relinquish it for the gold of a thousand Solomons! You would have proof of what I tell you? Well, some day perhaps you will!"

Henley started. The man had read his thoughts. It was the very question upon his lips.

"You are a mind reader!" cried Paul. "How did you know I was going to ask you that?"

Ah Ben made no answer; he did not even smile, but continued to gaze into the fire and blow little puffs of smoke toward the chimney.

"You referred just now to the prize-fighter," Paul resumed after a few minutes, "but I am going to squelch that argument."

"Yes," Ah Ben replied, now with his eyes half closed, "you are going to tell me that, although the man may have been battered and bruised, he really feels no pain, because of the unnatural excitement of the moment; but there you only rivet the argument against yourself; for I maintain—and not from theory, but from knowledge—that that very excitement is an exaltation of the spirit, which may be cultivated and relied upon to conquer pain and the ills of the flesh forever!"

"It would go far indeed if it could do all that, although I believe there is something in what you say, for in a small way I have seen it myself."

"Yes, we have all seen it in a small way; and does it not seem strange that men have never thought of cultivating it in a larger way, through the exercise of their will in controlling their minds and bodies? This exaltation of spirit is only attained through effort, or some great physical shock. It is the secret of all power; it conquers all pain, and makes disease impossible."

"Makes disease impossible!" cried Paul in astonishment.

"Yes," answered the elder man quietly. "This soul power, of which I speak, is the hidden akasa in all men—it is the man himself—and when once recognized, the body is relegated to its proper sphere as the servant, and not the master; then it is that man realizes his own power and supremacy over all things."

"But," persisted Henley, "if you go so far as to say that this occult or soul power can conquer disease, you would have us all living forever!"

"We do live forever," answered Ah Ben.

"Yes, after death; but I mean here!"

"*There is no such thing as death*!" remarked Ah Ben quietly, as if he were merely giving expression to a well-established scientific fact.

"And yet we see it about us every day," Paul replied.

"There you are wrong, for no man has ever seen that which never occurs!"

"You are quibbling with words," suggested Henley.

"There is a change at a certain period in a man's life, which, from ignorance, people have agreed to call death. But it is a misnomer, for man never dies. He goes right on living; and it is generally a considerable time before he realizes the change that has taken place in him. He would laugh at the word death, as understood upon earth, as indeed he frequently does, for he is far more alive than ever before."

"You speak as if you knew all this," said Paul. "One might almost imagine that you had been in the other world yourself."

"*Had been*!" exclaimed the old man with emphasis. "*I am in it now, and so are you. But there is a difference between us; I know that I am in it, because I can see it, and touch it, and hear it; while you are in it without knowing it.*"

There was an air of authority that impressed the hearer with the conviction of the speaker. This was not theory; it was the result of experience. There was a difference as vast as the night from the day. "I suppose, when I am dead, I shall know these things too," said Paul meditatively.

"No," answered Ah Ben, "not when you are dead, but when you have been born—when you have come into life."

"Pardon me," answered Paul, pondering on the man's strange assertion; "but this knowledge of yours is in demand more than all other knowledge. Positive information about the other world is what men have sought through all the ages; why do you not impart it to them?"

"Impart it!" exclaimed Ah Ben. "Can you explain to one who has been born blind what it is to see? Can you impart to such a man any true conception of the world in which he has always lived? But *couch* his eyes, remove the worthless film that has covered them, and for the first time he realizes the glorious world surrounding him. Likewise *couch* the body, remove the shell that covers the spirit, and it is born."

"I perceive, then, that it is only through death that most of us can hope to gain this knowledge."

"Death, if you prefer the word," said Ah Ben. "Yes, it is the death of the film over the eye that reveals the world to the blind; but I should hardly say that the man was dead because he had so entered into another existence."

"Would you mind telling me how it is that you have gained this knowledge in such obvious exception to the rule!"

"The power of the occult is dormant in all men," answered Ah Ben; "and as I have already said, may be developed slowly, through the exercise of the will, or suddenly, as in some great physical shock, and of a necessity comes to all in the event called death. Were I to tell you how *I* acquired this knowledge, Mr. Henley, it would startle you, far more than any exhibition of the power itself. No, I can not tell you; at least, not at present; perhaps some day you may be better prepared to hear it."

The spark in the hanging lamp had almost expired, and the fire was reduced to a mere handful of coals, casting an erubescent glow over the pew and its occupants. Ah Ben stretched his hand toward the chimney, and as he did so, a ball of misty light appeared against it, just below the mantel. It was ill defined and hazy, like the reflection a firefly will sometimes make against the ceiling of a darkened room; but it was fixed, and Paul was sure it had not been there a moment before.

"Do you see that?" asked the old man, breaking the silence.

"Yes," answered Paul; "and I was just wondering what it could be."

"Watch! and you will see."

They sat with their eyes fixed; but while Paul was staring into the mantel, Ah Ben was looking at him.

"Observe how it grows," and even as he spoke the strange illumination deepened, until it assumed the distinct and definite form of a lamp. Then the mantelpiece dissolved into nothingness, and Paul was staring through the chimney into a strange room, whose form and contents were dimly revealed by the curious lamp which occupied a table in the centre. Two persons sat at this table, the one a woman, the other a boy, and near at hand was an English army officer. The woman was small, with dark eyes and hair, and a skin the color of tan bark. Her head was bowed forward and rested upon her arms, which were crossed upon the table. The man was looking down at her with a troubled expression, and in a minute he stooped forward and kissed the top of her head; he then turned suddenly and left the room. The scene was distinct, although the outer part of the room was in shadow. Presently the woman threw herself to the floor with a heart-rending shriek, and Paul started up, exclaiming:

"What has happened? She will wake everybody in the house!"

He bounded to his feet; but as he did so, the lamp in the strange room went out, and the chimney closed over the scene, leaving him with his old surroundings. Looking up at Ah Ben, he said:

"I must have fallen asleep. I've been dreaming."

"Not at all," answered Ah Ben. "You've been quite as wide awake as I have, and we've been looking at the same thing."

Paul demanded the proof, which the old man gave by telling him what he had seen in every detail.

"Then it's magic!" said Henley, "for surely no room can be visible through that chimney."

"That," answered Ah Ben, "is mere assertion, which you can never prove."

"Do you mean to tell me that the thing was real? There is a secret about this house which I do not understand!"

His manner was excited. He felt that he had been the dupe of the man before him, the prey to some clever trick; the thing was too preposterous, too unreasonable.

"Be calm," said Ah Ben; "there is nothing in this that should disturb you. The room has disappeared from our sight, and will no more trouble us. Shall we have another pipe?"

The words had an instantaneous effect, so that Paul resumed his seat and pipe, as if nothing had happened. For several minutes he sat silently gazing at vacancy, and listening to the north wind as it moaned through the old pines. He was trying to account for what he had seen, but could not. The mystery was deepening into an overpowering gloom. The house, with its eccentric inmates; the girl Dorothy, with her freaks and manner of living; the odd circumstance of the stairway in his closet; these, and other things, flashed upon his memory in a confused jumble, and seemed as inexplicable as the vision just witnessed through the chimney.

Suddenly a thought struck him. Could this last have been hypnotism? He put the question straight to Ah Ben. The man passed his withered hand over his face thoughtfully as he answered:

"Hypnotism, Mr. Henley, is a name that is used in the West for a condition that has been known in the East for thousands of years as the underlying principle of *all phenomena.*"

"And what is that condition?" Paul inquired.

"*Sympathetic vibration,*" answered the elder man.

"Vibration of what?" asked Paul.

"Of the mind," said Ah Ben. "The condition of the universal mind vibrating in our material plane, or within the range of our physical senses, is represented in the trees and the rocks, in the earth and the stars. Our physical senses, being attuned to his form of vibration, are in sympathy with it, and apprehend all its phenomena. There is but one mind, of which man is a part. Thought is a product of mind.

Thought is real, and, when sufficiently concentrated, becomes tangible and visible to those who can be brought into sympathy with its vibrations. There is but one primal substance, which is mind. Mind creates all things out of itself; therefore, to change the world we look at, it is only necessary to change our minds."

"Let me ask if what I saw was hypnotism?" repeated Henley. "I ask this, first, because I know it is impossible to see through a brick wall, even if there should be such a room in the house; and, secondly, because I cannot believe that I was dreaming, consequently the thing could not have been real."

"Hypnotism is a good enough word," answered Ah Ben; "but that which men generally understand by the real, and that which they consider the unreal, are not so far apart as they suppose. You say the room was not real, and yet you saw it; had you wished, you might have touched it, which is certainly all the evidence you have of the existence of the room in which we are now sitting. Hypnotism is not a cause of hallucination, as is commonly supposed, but of fact. Its effects are not illusory, but real. Perhaps it would be more correct to say that they are *as real* as anything else, and that *all* the phenomena of nature are mere illusions of the senses, which they undoubtedly are. But whichever side we take, all appearances are the result of the same general cause—that of mental vibration. Matter has no real existence."

Paul was meditating on what he had seen and what he was now hearing. Ah Ben's words were endowed with an added force by the vision of the mysterious room.

"When you tell me that there is practically no difference between the real and the unreal, and that matter has no real existence, I must confess to some perplexity," observed Henley.

Ah Ben looked up and smoothed the furrows in his withered cheek thoughtfully for a minute before he answered:

"Unfortunately, Mr. Henley, language is not absolute or final in its power to convey thought, and the best we can do is to use it as carefully as possible to express ourselves, which we can only hope to do approximately. Therefore when I say that a thing is hot or cold, or hard or soft, I only mean that it is so by comparison with certain other things; and when I say that matter has no existence, I mean that it has no independent existence—no existence outside of the mind that brought it into being. I mean that it was formed by mind, formed out of mind, and that it continues to exist in mind as a part of mind. I mean that it is an appearance objective to our point of consciousness on the material plane; but inasmuch as it was formed by thought, it can be reformed by thought, which could never be if it existed independently of thought. It is real in the sense of apparent objectivity, and not real in the sense of independent objectivity, and yet it affects us in precisely the same manner as if it were independent of thought. What, then, is the difference between matter as viewed from the Idealist's or the Materialist's point of view? At first there is apparently none, but a deeper insight will show us that the difference is vast and radical, for in the one case the tree or the chair that I am looking at, owing its very existence to mind, is governed by mind, which could never be did they exist as separate and distinct entities. Therefore I say with perfect truth that matter does not exist in the one sense, and yet that it does exist in the other. I dream of a green field; a beautiful landscape, never before beheld; I awake and it is gone. Where was that enchanting scene? I can tell you: for it was in the mind, where everything else is. But upon waking I have changed my mind, and the scene has vanished. Thus it is with the Adept of the East, with the Yoghis, the Pundit, the Rishis, and the common Fakir; through the power of hypnotism they alter the condition of the subject's mind, and with it his world has likewise undergone a change. You say this is not real, that it is merely illusion; but in reply I would say that these illusions have been subjected to the severest tests; their reality has been certified to by every human sense, and when an illusion responds to the sense of both sight and touch, when the sense of sight is corroborated by that of touch, or by any other of the five senses, what *better* evidence have we of the existence of those things we are all agreed to call real? Yes, I know what you are about to say, you object upon the ground that only a small minority are witnesses of the marvels of Eastern magic; but you are wrong, for I have seen hundreds of men in a public square all eye-witnesses to precisely the same occult phenomena at once. Now if certain hundreds could be so impressed, why not other hundreds? And with a still more powerful hypnotizer, why could not a majority—nay, all of those in a certain district, a certain State, a certain country, *in the world*—be made to see and feel things which now, and to us, have no existence? In that case, Mr. Henley, would it be the majority or the minority who were deceived? *All is mind,* and the hypnotizer merely alters it."

"You said just now," answered Paul, "that matter, being mind, was governed by mind, and that the tree or chair before me, owing its existence to mind, is subject to that mind; do you mean by that to say that the existence of that sofa, as a sofa, may be transformed into something else by mental action alone?"

"I do," said Ah Ben, "under certain conditions; namely, the condition called hypnotism. On this material plane we are imprisoned; the will is not free to operate upon its environment, but in the spiritual state this dependence and slavery to the appearances we call realities is cast aside; the will becomes free and controls its own environment—in short, we are out of prison. But even here, Mr. Henley, by practicing the self-control we were speaking of, the will becomes so powerful that it can sometimes break through the bondage of matter, which, after all, is no more real than the stuff a dream is made of, and mold its prison walls into any form it chooses; in which case, of course, it is no longer a prison, and the other world is achieved without the change called death!"

"And why do you call it a prison, if no more real than a dream?"

"Have you ever had the nightmare? If so, you must know that your will was insufficient to free you from the horrid scene that had taken such forcible hold of you. Was the nightmare real or not?"

Paul was silent for several minutes. He could not deny the reality of the scene through the chimney, for it had the same forceful existence to him as anything in life. Ah Ben, seeing that he was still puzzling himself over the problem of mind and matter, the puzzle of life, the great sphinx riddle of the ages, said:

"Let me ask you a question, Mr. Henley—I might say several questions—which may possibly tend to throw a little light upon this subject, and perhaps convince you that matter is really mind."

"Ask as many as you like."

"Pantheism," continued Ah Ben, "is scoffed at by many people calling themselves Christians as being idolatrous, and yet to me it is the most ennobling of all creeds. Without knowing anything of your religious faith, I would first ask if you believe in God?"

Paul answered affirmatively.

"Do you look upon him as a personal Deity—I mean as an exaggerated man in size and power—or as a Spirit?"

"As a Spirit," Paul replied.

"Very well, then; do you believe that Spirit is infinite or finite?"

"Infinite."

"Then, if it is infinite, there can be no part of space in which it does not exist."

"That is my idea also."

"If, then, that Spirit exists everywhere, it must penetrate all matter; in fact, all matter must, in its very essence, be a part of it; it must be formed out of the very substance of this infinite Spirit or Mind. Hence all is mind!"

"That seems clear enough," said Paul; "in which case it seems to me that we are a part of God ourselves, and God being spirit, we must be spirits now."

"Of course we are," answered Ah Ben; "as I have already told you, we are in the spiritual world now, although much of it is screened from our view, because we are temporarily imprisoned in a lower vibratory plane, called matter."

Ah Ben arose, and procuring candles, which he lighted by the expiring fire, the men went to their beds.

6

It was past midnight, and the house quiet, when Paul determined to have another look at the mysterious door at the foot of his closet stairs. He had sat for more than an hour before his bedroom fire, after bidding Ah Ben good-night, to make sure that the inmates of Guir House had retired; and as not a sound had been heard since locking his door, he sincerely hoped they were asleep. Before descending into the noisome depths, however, he concluded to climb up into his window, and have another look at the beautiful panorama of mountain and woodland shimmering in the meagre light of a hazy sky and a moon past full. The uncertain outline of a distant horizon; the interminable stretch of forest, which bore away upon every hand; the rugged heights, now soft and colorless; the aromatic smell of pine and fir; the distant murmur of falling water; and the assonant whispering of wind in the tree tops, had all become strangely fascinating to him, more so than such things had ever been before. "Never was a house so situated, so lost to the world, so tightly held in the lap of unregenerate nature," thought Paul; "no laugh of child, no shout of man, no bark of dog, nor bellowing beast to break the stillness of the midnight air; an impenetrable, imperturbable, and silent wilderness shuts out the busy world, as we know it, forever and forever. It is a fitting place for such witchery as the old man seems master of, and I do not wonder that he has chosen it for his home; but the girl—the poor girl!—she must get away!" He closed the window, and prepared for his descent into the well.

Removing his shoes, he put on a pair of soft felt slippers, and then, with candle in his hand, a box of matches and a revolver in his pocket, entered the closet, and opened the scuttle in the floor. A mouldy smell rose upon the air, and Henley recoiled at the thought of what might be in waiting below. He had not the slightest idea of how he should open the door at the bottom, but would make a careful study of the situation, hoping that a solution of the difficulty would present itself. The steps creaked dismally as he placed his weight upon them, and it was necessary to use extreme caution to avoid breaking through the more rotten ones. He had not descended more than a dozen, when there was a terrible crash above his head, and he found himself in absolute darkness. The trap had fallen as upon the previous night, he having forgotten to fasten it back, and the wind had blown out his candle. Henley hastened back up the stairs, fearful lest the noise had waked some one in the house, and without relighting his candle threw himself upon the bed to await developments. After listening for some minutes, and hearing nothing, he became convinced that no one had been disturbed; and so, creeping out of bed, and lighting his candle by the dying embers in the fireplace, started in afresh. This time he was careful to fasten back the scuttle door, and in doing so discovered that one of the great iron hinges was loose. It was more than two feet long, and with very little difficulty he managed to wrench it off, thinking it might possibly be of service in forcing the door at the bottom. He was careful this time to let the scuttle down quietly after him, thinking it safer to do this than to prop it open.

The bottom was reached in safety after the usual doleful crunching and creaking of the timber, and Paul sat down on the bottom step, with his candle, to rest and quiet himself, before proceeding with his work upon the door. A dead stillness reigned all about him, broken only by the occasional resettling of the steps above his head, but which, to his excited brain, was like the report of a pistol; still even this ceased in a few minutes, and the silence was undisturbed. He now made a careful examination of the door. It was very heavy, and solid. Holding his candle close against the crack, he could see, to his surprise, that it was bolted upon the inside. Placing his ear close against the keyhole, he listened, but it was silent as a tomb within; and how the door became fastened upon the inside was inexplicable, unless indeed there was another outlet, which from his examination of the building had seemed improbable. Then, taking out his knife, he stuck it into the wood in various directions to ascertain the condition of its preservation. The door itself was in an excellent state; but in examining the lintel, the blade of his knife suddenly sank into the rotten wood up to the handle. Here, then, was the place to begin operations, and fortunately it was on the side from which the door opened. Henley had soon dug away a great segment of decayed wood, exposing the bolt clearly to view. Then taking the hinge which he had brought with him, and slipping the small end between the bolt and the frame of the door, he used it as a lever to pry against the bolt within. The iron was so old and rusty, and his purchase so poor, that he only succeeded in making a rasping sound where the two metals scraped against each other, and so stopped, discouraged. Presently he bethought him of his handkerchief, which he wrapped carefully around the end of the hinge, and thus not only gained a better purchase, increasing his leverage, but was able to operate without the slightest sound. It was a long time before the bolt moved, but to his intense gratification it did move at last, and Henley took a fresh grip upon his hinge. Backward and forward he worked his lever, and with each turn the old bolt slipped back a little. At last he could see the end of it, and then it was clear of the frame entirely. He had expected no difficulty in opening the door when the hinge was once slipped, but to his surprise it was still immovable. He pulled and tugged and pushed, but it would not budge; then suddenly, just as he was about to give up, it came tumbling down upon him, so that he was barely able to save it from falling against the stairs with a terrible crash, but fortunately caught it upon his shoulder, and lowered it to the floor without a sound. Imagine his surprise in going to what he now believed to be the open portal, to find that the doorway had been bricked up from within, and that the door itself had simply been the back of a solid wall. Naturally, he was disappointed at finding himself no nearer the inner chamber than before. A careful examination of the masonry showed that the work of bricking up the entrance had undoubtedly been done from the other side, and after the door had been closed and bolted. This was evidenced from the fact that there was no mortar next the door, against the smooth inner surface of which the bricks had been closely laid. Henley worked his hinge between some of the looser joints, and found, just as he expected, that the mortar had been laid from within. By degrees he managed to wedge one of the bricks out of its place, and then pulled it bodily from the wall. The inner surface was plastered over. He tried another, which he got out more easily, and it told the same tale. Then he went to work in earnest, and had soon dug a hole large enough to admit his body. Leaning over into the aperture, with his candle at arm's length, the place looked dark and empty, with faint masses of lighter shadow. Then, with a certain indescribable awe, Henley commenced crawling through the breach. Stepping upon an earthern floor, he found himself in a vault-like chamber—damp, mouldy, and foul of atmosphere. He glanced hurriedly about, and then turned to examine the wall through which he had come. Just as he had surmised, the bricks had been laid from the inner side, and plastered over within. The person who had done the work must have had some other means of escape. This set him to wondering where the other entrance could be, and to a careful search around the wall; but there was no door, no window, nor opening of any kind. How had the work been done? While he was wondering, he stumbled over something in the floor, and, recovering, threw back his head, holding his candle high above it. He was startled by the sight of what appeared to be four shadowy human faces, looking directly at him from above. Instinctively he sought his revolver, but before drawing it perceived that what he had taken for living people were simply four portraits, of the most remarkable character he had ever beheld. Paul stared in bewilderment at the sight before him. The pictures were so old, their canvases so rotten and mildewed and stained with the accumulated fungi of time and darkness that it was only by degrees that the intention of the artist became manifest. In the hall and other apartments of the old house, Henley thought he had seen the most original and inexplicable pictures ever painted; but here, buried forever from the sight of human eyes, were the most dreadful countenances ever transcribed from life or the imagination of man. Torture was clearly depicted upon each face; but not torture alone, for horror, fright, and mental agony were strangely blended in each. Not a face that looked down upon him from those antiquated frames but bore that agonized, heart-broken, terrified expression. Paul was paralyzed; a kind of mesmeric spell held him to the spot, so that he could not remove his eyes from the uncanny scene before him. Then a wild desire to be rid of the place forever seized him, and he stepped backward. At the same minute he observed for the first time what looked like some faded letters painted upon the wall directly beneath the four mysterious portraits. Examining these with his candle, he saw that they formed the words:

"*The last of the Guirs.*"

"No wonder Dorothy said that she was afraid of them," Paul reflected; "their portraits alone would drive me mad." He took another long searching look; and as his eyes grew accustomed to the faded coloring, he observed how cleverly the work had been done. Evidently the pictures had been painted from life, though under what circumstances Henley could never imagine. The faces were all those of a feminine type; they were of young women, apparently but little more than girls, and each with this life-like, though dreadful expression. As Paul stood marveling and wondering, a new interest seized him. At first he could not quite understand what it was, but it became stronger and better defined, he knew, for he recognized one of the faces. Yes, there could be no mistake about it; the picture on the left was a *portrait of Dorothy herself.* Henley rubbed his eyes, and looked again and again; he could not believe their evidence, but they had not deceived him. He tried to make himself believe that it was the likeness of some ancestor, to whom she had a strange resemblance; but, despite the look of pain, it could be no other than Dorothy, and indeed this very expression helped to heighten the likeness, for had he not seen a similar expression at the breakfast table? The longer he gazed at it, the more convinced he became that this was a portrait of Miss Guir. At last, thoroughly mystified, he turned away, intending to leave this grewsome chamber of horrors forever; but now for the first time the heap of rubbish in the center of the floor engaged his attention. Taking his hinge, he stirred up the mass; some shreds of cloth, which fell to pieces on being touched, and beneath them some human bones. This was all, but it was enough; and overwhelmed with horror, Henley rushed out of the room, bounding through the aperture he had made in the wall, and up the rickety stairs into his own bed chamber. He carefully closed the scuttle, heaped some firewood upon it, shut the closet door and fastened it securely from without. He then built up a roaring fire, lit another candle, and sat meditating over what he had seen until the dawn of day. When the light of the sun came streaming into his room, he undressed and went to bed.

Whatever may have been Mr. Henley's suspicions concerning the implication of the Guirs with the crime which he could no longer doubt had been committed in their house, they were promptly dispelled, so far as the young lady was concerned, upon meeting Dorothy at the breakfast table. Her innocent though serious face was a direct rebuke to any distrust he might have entertained; and he even doubted if she had any knowledge of the state of things he had discovered in the vault. This, of course, only added to the mystery; nor was Mr. Henley's self-esteem fortified by the memory of how unscrupulously he had become the guest of these people, and of how equivocal had been his treatment of their hospitality. All this, however, related to the past, and, as he felt, could not be now undone. He must act to the best of his ability in the extraordinary position in which he found himself.

After breakfast they walked again into the garden, and while Paul smoked his cigarette, meditatively, Dorothy gathered flowers for the house. There was an earnestness in everything that she did, quite unusual in a girl of her age, and at times her manner was grave and sad, but strangely attractive, nevertheless. When she had completed her labors in the garden, she came and seated herself beside him.

"Some day, Paul, we'll have a cheerier home than this; won't we?" she said, looking wistfully up at the quaint old pile before them.

"I don't think we could have a more romantic one," he answered; and then, hoping to elicit an explanatory answer, added, "but why should Guir House not seem cheerful to you?"

"I don't know; it has always been gloomy; don't you think so?"

"Not having known it always, Dorothy, I am not in a position to judge; but it will always be the sweetest place on earth to me, because I met you here for the first time."

"Yes, I know; but you must not forget your promise."

She seemed nervous and anxious concerning his fulfillment of it.

"And do you suppose that I could ever forget anything you asked me? No, Dorothy, while you will it, I am your slave; but, as I told you before, you exert such a strange power over me that you could make me hate and fear you. I don't know why this should be so, but I feel it!"

"Hush!" she said, extending her outstretched hand toward his mouth; "do not talk in that way; you frighten me; for, O Paul! I was just beginning to hope that in you I had found a friend who would never shrink away from me. Do not tell me that you will ever become afraid of me like the others. I could not bear it."

"I shrink! God forbid," he answered, "but tell me why are other people afraid of you? You mystify me."

"Because I am different—so different from them!"

"I'm quite sure of that," he replied, "else I should never have come to love you within an hour of meeting you."

She did not smile; she did not even look up at him, but sat gazing at nothing, with countenance as solemn and imperturbable as that of a Sphinx.

"How am I ever to understand you, Dorothy, you seem such a riddle?" said Paul presently.

"You will never understand me," she answered with a sigh, "No one ever has understood me, and you will be just like the rest!"

"But you will never let me be afraid of you, like the others, will you?" he exclaimed half in earnest.

"I don't know; others are; why should not you be?"

She was still staring into vacancy, with her hands clasped, and Paul thought he detected a little, just a little, of the same expression he had seen in the portrait. He started, and Dorothy saw him.

"What is the matter?" she inquired, looking around at him for the first time.

"Nothing; only you looked so dreadfully in earnest, you startled me."

"But surely you would not be startled by so simple a thing as that!"

"Why not? I am only human," he answered.

"Yes, but I am sure there was something else. Now tell me, was there not?"

"Why, how strangely you talk!" he replied, searching her face for an explanation. "Of course there wasn't; why should there be?"

She leaned back, apparently still in doubt as to his assertion, while her countenance grew even more grave than before. Henley was puzzled, and while Dorothy had not ceased to charm him, he was conscious of a very slight uneasiness in her presence. This, however, wore off a little later when they went together for a stroll in the forest. The girl's extreme delicacy of appearance, her abstracted, melancholy manner, and sincerity of expression, both attracted and perplexed Paul, and kept him constantly at work endeavoring to solve her character and form some conception of the mystery of her life. He had not yet had even the courage to ask her if Ah Ben were her father, dreading to expose himself as an impostor and be ordered from the place, which, despite his discovery of the previous night, he could only regard as an unmitigated hardship in the present state of his feelings; and so he had let the hours slip by, constantly hoping that something would occur to explain the whole situation to him. And yet nothing had occurred, and now upon the third day he was as grossly ignorant of the causes which had produced his strange environment as at the moment of his arrival.

"One thing I do not understand," Paul observed, as they wandered over the vari-colored leaves, side by side; "it is why you should be so anxious to leave this ideal spot."

"Have I not told you that it is because I am out of my element; because I am avoided; because I have not a friend far nor near! Oh, Paul, you do not know what it is to be alone in the world!"

"And do you believe that a simple change of locality would alter all this?" he asked.

She paused for a moment before answering, and then, looking down upon the ground, said as if with some effort:

"No, not that alone."

"What then, Dorothy?" he asked with solicitude.

"I have already told you," she replied without looking up. "Oh, Paul, what a short memory you must have!"

"Of course I understand that we are to be married," he responded hastily, "but how can that alter the situation? Dorothy, if we have not found congenial friends in that position in life in which God or nature has placed us, how can we hope to make them in another? Do you not think there may be some deeper reason than simple locality and single blessedness? Would it not be natural to look for the cause in the individual?"

"Undoubtedly you are right," she answered, "but your premises do not apply to my case, for neither God nor nature ever intended that I should live this life. Oh, Paul, believe me when I tell you that I know whereof I speak. Do not judge me as you would another; some day you may know, but I can not tell you now."

She spoke pleadingly, as imploring to be released from some awful incubus which it was impossible to explain. Paul listened in deep perplexity, and swore that the powers of heaven and earth should never come between them. So different was she from any girl that he had ever seen, that her very eccentricity bound him to her with a magic spell. When he had again asked her if Ah Ben would oppose their marriage, or indeed if any one else would, she declared that no human being would raise a voice against it.

"Then what is to hinder us?" he asked; "I am poor, but I can support you; not perhaps in such luxury as you are accustomed to, but I can give you a home; and if you are so unhappy here, why submit to unnecessary delay?"

He had become impassioned and enthused by the girl's strange influence over him.

"True, Paul, there are none to hinder us," she replied seriously, "that is, no one but—but— "

She paused, not knowing how to proceed.

"Then there is some one," cried Paul earnestly. "I thought as much. Who might the gentleman be?"

"Yourself!" exclaimed Dorothy, her eyes still fixed upon the ground.

"Myself!" shouted he in amazement. "Do you mean to say that I should oppose my own marriage with the girl I love?"

"You might," she answered demurely, casting a side glance up at him, and allowing the very faintest, saddest kind of smile to rest for an instant upon her face.

"Well!" said Paul, "I do not suppose you will explain what you mean, but it would be only natural that I should like to know."

"I only mean," she replied, resuming her meditative attitude, "that you do not know me; that you neither know who nor what I am. If I did not love you, I might deceive and entrap you, but not under the circumstances."

Later they returned to the house.

7

It was not until Mr. Henley had made another and longer visit to the dark room that he became convinced beyond all doubt that the work of sealing up the place had been done from within, and that there was, and had been, no other outlet but that through which he had entered. To suppose that the main wall of the house had been closed in at a later period would be preposterous, and for manifest reasons. His examination of the room's interior had been most thorough and exhaustive. The place was smoothly plastered upon the inside, and even the mason's trowel had been found upon the floor within, so that it became at once evident that those who had done the work had been self-immured. Although the reason for such an act was utterly beyond his comprehension, Paul felt a certain satisfaction in having reached this conclusion, as it showed the impossibility of Dorothy's being in any way implicated in the affair. It seemed even possible that she was ignorant of it. But this discovery in no wise lessened the mystery; it rather increased it.

A few evenings after Paul's decision regarding the self-immurement of those discovered in the vault, he and Ah Ben were again enjoying their pipes by the great fireplace in the hall. The elder man was generally disposed to conversation at this hour; and after Dorothy had retired, Paul alluded to the strange scene he had witnessed through the chimney, and expressed a desire to learn something of occultism. Taking his long-stemmed pipe from his lips, the old man gazed earnestly into the fire. He seemed to be thinking of what to say, and to be drawing inspiration from the glowing embers and dancing flames before him. At last he spoke:

"Occultism, Mr. Henley, is difficult—nay, almost impossible—to explain to a layman; or if explained, remains incomprehensible; and yet a child may acquire its secrets by its individual efforts. Spiritual power comes to those who seek it in proper mood, but, injudiciously exercised, may cause insanity."

"Nevertheless," urged Paul, "if you won't consider me a trifler, I should like to see a further manifestation of the power."

Ah Ben looked at him compassionately.

"Pardon me, Mr. Henley," he said, "but it is not always well to gratify our curiosity upon such a subject; but if you seriously wish it, and can believe in me as an honest and honorable custodian of the power, and will prepare yourself for a serious mental shock, I will show you something."

"Before proceeding," said Paul, "I should like to ask you a question. Was the room I saw through the chimney a real room? I mean had it any material existence upon earth?"

"Most assuredly. It was a scene in my early childhood, and originated in the Valley of the Jhelum, in the Punjab. The officer and lady were my parents. It was the last time I ever saw them. I was the boy."

"May I ask how it is possible to reproduce a scene so long passed out of existence, and which took place so many thousand miles away?"

"Easily told, but not so easily understood by one whose mind has never been trained to think in these occult channels," answered the elder man; "for to understand the thing at all, you must first divest your mind of time and space as outside entities, for these are in reality but modes of thought, and have only such value as we give them. India, doubtless, seems very far to you, but to one whose powers of will have been sufficiently developed, it is no farther than the wall of this room. So it is with time. How can we see that which no longer exists? But a little reflection will show us that even on the physical plane we see that which does not exist every day of our lives. Look at the stars. The light by which some of them are recognized has been millions of years in transit, so that we do not behold them as they are tonight, but as they were at that remote period of time; meanwhile they may have been wrecked and scattered in meteoric dust."

"But that is hardly an explanation of the scene referred to," answered Paul. "Whenever I direct my eyes in the right quarter, the stars are visible; whether they be actually there or not, they are there to me; but not so with the vision of the room. In my normal condition there is no room there, while in my normal condition the stars are always there."

"True, and because your normal condition is sympathetically attuned to the vibrations of starlight. Your consciousness is located in your brain, and so long as those vibrations continue to strike with sufficient force upon the optic nerve, you will be conscious of the light. But suppose the machinery of your body were finer—suppose your senses were absolutely in accord with those vibratory movements, instead of only partially so—do you not know that the starlight would reveal far more than it now does? Then you would see not only the light, but the scenes that are carried in the light, but which by reason of their obtuseness can not penetrate your senses. Were this improvement in men really achieved, our conceptions of time and space would be modified, and the condition of other worlds as plainly seen as our own."

"Yes," said Paul, determined to follow up the original question, "but what of a scene that occurred in this world some years ago, and whose light vibrations would require but the fraction of a second to reach our point of consciousness—no matter where situated on earth—and which vibrations have long since passed beyond the reach of man, and been lost in infinite space?"

"Nothing is ever lost, and infinite space is but a phase of infinite mind. All that is necessary to review such a picture is to change our point of consciousness from the brain to a point in space or *mind*, where the vibratory movement is still in progress. In other words, to overtake the scene by transposing our consciousness. Granted these powers, which are born of the soul, and we may behold any event in history with the clearness of its original force. Man is mind, and mind is one; but all mind is not self-conscious. The consciousness of mind is in spots, as it were, and here its consciousness is fixed in a spot called brain, where with most men it remains until the will, or some abnormal condition or the event called death, liberates it from its prison. You believe that with your God, the scenes of yesterday, to-day, and forever are alike visible?"

"Even admitting all that you say," answered Paul, "I can not see how it was that I, who have no such power, could see clearly an event in your life."

"Again the power of sympathetic vibration. The scene was reflected from my mind to yours."

"But you just now said there was but one mind."

"Perhaps then it would be more correct to say, from my point of consciousness to yours; or, to be still more accurate, to say that the intensity of my thoughts struck a sympathetic chord in yours, and vibrated through you as one consciousness. Without undue familiarity, Mr. Henley, I have found in you a responsive temperament. There are few men I can not influence, and with some the effort is trifling."

Paul was interested, and sat quietly reflecting upon what he had heard. Naturally the ideas were not so clear as they would have been had he given more thought to the conditions of spirituality, which for so many years had been a part of Ah Ben's existence, and which state was as familiar to him as the body in which he appeared. Time and reflection alone, as this strange man had declared, could bring one to comprehend and realize a condition of existence so totally differing from that of our material plane. The inability of language to express that of which we have no parallel, and of which we can not conceive, is a grave obstacle to our understanding; but the man was ever ready to exert himself to make the matter clear when he found his listener interested.

"If I am not tiring you," continued Paul, "I should like to call your attention to another point. You said that nothing was absolute; that all was relative; and yet when it comes to fixed measures, I think you must admit that this is not so. For example, a mile is a mile, and a mile must always be a mile under every conceivable condition. Am I not right?"

"At first thought it would seem so," answered Ah Ben. "A mile certainly appears to be an absolute unchanging quantity of so many feet, which must always and under every circumstance affect us in the same way; and yet a little reflection will show that this can not be so, and that a mile, after all, is only fixed so long as our mind is fixed. In other words, it is a mental conception, and relative to other mental conceptions. Let us, for example, suppose that the world and all its contents, and, in fact, the entire universe, were exactly twice as large as it is, the mile would then be twice as long as it is now; and that which we *now* call a mile would only make the impression of half as much distance as it now does. And so with all material conditions; I say *material*, for in the spiritual life we see these things more truly as they are, and not as they appear. There is but one class of facts which is absolute. I speak of the emotions. These are the realities of life—the soul qualities. Could we measure *love*, *hate*, or *happiness*, the standard would be fixed."

"Do not forget your promise to show me something more of your power in the region of occultism," said Henley, "for I am greatly interested."

"I will keep my word, but I warn you to prepare for a shock!"

"I am ready, and should like nothing better than to witness an example of your greatest power!"

The old man looked solemn, and then slowly answered:

"You shall be gratified. It is now past midnight. Dorothy is asleep, and it is a fitting time. If you will follow me to my own room, I will show you a mystery."

For a moment Paul hesitated. The thought of following this strange man at such an hour into the realm of the unknown, to investigate the supernatural, was uncanny, and he half wished he had not made the request. He knew the man to be no trifler. That which he promised, he would surely perform. Then, procuring a candle, Ah Ben led the way.

They walked along the narrow passage at the rear, Ah Ben stopping to close the door quietly behind them. They then mounted a still narrower stairway at the back, Paul following closely. Presently they entered a passage which led in the opposite direction from Henley's bedchamber, and then, turning sharply to the right, found a narrow hallway which terminated in a door. Here the men stopped.

"I am going to take you into my sanctum, and you must not be surprised if you find things different from the ordinary. The circumstances of my life have set me apart from most men; and if my surroundings are at variance with theirs, you must set it down to these facts."

Here he opened the door.

The room was lighted with the same lamp that Paul had seen through the chimney. There were odd-looking things, such as a skeleton with artificial eyes; a glass manikin with a reddish fluid that meandered through his body in thread-like streams; a horoscope and a globe, suspended from the ceiling, with the signs of the Zodiac. Various old parchments, covered with quaint cabalistic figures, were tacked against the walls. In a cabinet, embellished with hieroglyphics, stood another human form, a mummy wonderfully preserved.

"Here we are alone," said Ah Ben; "it is the quietest hour of the night, and therefore we are least apt to be disturbed."

"And what do you propose?" asked Paul with a misgiving he was loth to admit.

"Whatever you may desire, Mr. Henley; for you must know that which is born of spirit is not subject to the restrictions of matter. But remember that all is natural; there is no supernatural, and therefore no cause for alarm."

Ah Ben led the way to the window, and having drawn aside the curtain, threw up the sash. To Henley's amazement they walked directly through the open casement and found themselves upon a broad stone terrace in the glaring light of day. Beneath them lay a city of marvelous beauty, whose streets were lined with palaces, surrounded by their own parks, and whose inhabitants were walking in and about the shaded thoroughfares, or resting in the public seats beside them. The change was so sudden, so bewildering, that Paul drew back, his hand pressed against his head; whereupon Ah Ben took him by the arm and said:

"There is nothing here to alarm you. Come, let us descend these steps, and walk through the town!"

The voice and touch of the man reassured him.

Walking down the broad stone steps, they found themselves in a noble avenue lined with trees and adorned with sparkling fountains. Everywhere the people looked happy. There was neither hurry nor effort, but the grandest monuments to human action were visible upon every hand. Such palaces of dazzling marble; such lace-like carvings in stone; such noble terraces and gardens; and open to all the world alike.

"See," said Ah Ben, "the people here are of one mind. There is no wrangling nor struggling for place. These palaces are the property of the public; and why should they not be, since man's unity is understood? Exclusiveness is the result of ignorance, but privacy and seclusion may even be better enjoyed in the conditions prevailing here than in our own state of existence, and because of the unlimited power and material to draw upon. No man can crowd another after he has come to realize that all is mind, and that mind is infinite."

"But where is Guir House, and the estate?" inquired Paul, feeling as if the whole thing were an incomprehensible illusion.

"They have not been disturbed," the old man answered. "They are where they always were, *in the minds of those who perceive them, and upon whose plane they exist*."

"It is too utterly bewildering. These things appear as real as any I ever saw."

"Appear! They *are as real*. Let us go into one of these bazars, and see what the people are doing."

They turned through an open doorway resplendent with burnished metal and sculpture to where great corridors, halls, and galleries, stocked with properties and merchandise of every description, were crowded with people. No one was in attendance; and those who came and went, carried with them what they pleased. No money was passed, nor did compensation of any kind seem forthcoming. "If anything strikes your fancy, take it," said Ah Ben. "All things here are free, and yet everything is paid for."

Paul asked for an explanation, which Ah Ben gave as follows:

"The city before you is located in the year 3,000, more than a thousand years in advance of our time. It is called *Levachan*, and will appear upon earth about 700 years hence; in about four hundred years from which time it will attain the size and splendor you now behold. We here see it in its spiritual state, which precedes and follows all material forms. It will begin its descent into matter, through the minds of physical man, about the time I have mentioned. It is merely a type of a class toward which we are tending, and I show it to you that you may see the vast strides we shall have made by that time. In the state of society in which we find ourselves, compensation is made by a system of absolute freedom in exchange. Here, if a man wants a coat, he takes it, and the owner reimburses himself from the great reservoir of the world's goods, which is open to all men as integral parts of a unit."

"What check have you upon the unreasoning rapacity of a thief, who will take ten times as much as he requires?"

"The system operates directly against the development of that trait. Here, men are only too anxious to have their goods admired and taken; for, being certain of their own maintenance, they feel a pride in contributing to that of others, and there is no temptation to take that which can not be kept, since his neighbor has equal right to take from him an idle surplus. Here the laws are the reverse of ours, for here a man is encouraged in the taking, but never in the holding. Wealth is measured by what a man disburses; hence all are anxious to part with their individual property for the advancement of the commonwealth, knowing that the *one* can only thrive when the many are prosperous."

They continued their walk amid the marvelous wealth that surrounded them. There were fabrics of untold value; jewels of indescribable splendor; men, women, and children with strangely eager faces. They seated themselves upon revolving chairs in the midst of a great space to watch the glittering show.

"But tell me what it all means," inquired Paul. "I feel as if it were a dream, and yet I am absolutely certain that it is not."

"You are right; it is not a dream. Levachan is as real as New York, Boston, or Chicago, although invisible to men of earth. Its inhabitants are as conscious of their existence as you and I are of ours. They are quite as alive to their history and probable destiny as any well educated citizen of America or Europe."

"But where is Guir House, and all it contained?" repeated Henley, unable to understand.

"Nothing has been changed by this any more than if you were in your bed dreaming it all. But to you it is incomprehensible, as I told you it would be, because your mind has never been trained to think in these realms."

"No," answered Paul, turning uneasily in his chair, dazed by the marvelous pageant that moved constantly about them. "No, I admit that it has not, and that the whole thing is utterly beyond me; and this, none the less, because I am aware that one of the fundamental facts of nature is that two things can not occupy the same space at the same time. My previous education, instead of helping me, makes the situation more difficult. The Guir estate and this city can not both be here at once; of that I am sure."

"That is a mere assumption on the part of materialists," answered Ah Ben. "Not only two things, but ten million things, can occupy the same space at the same time; for what is space, and what is time? They are mental conditions, as are all the phenomena of nature. Even your scientist will tell you that the infinite ether penetrates all substances, and that cast-steel or a diamond contains as much of this mysterious element as any other space of equal size. The varying vibrations of this ether, or universal akasa, make the world and all that is in it; and these vibrations are interpenetrable and non-obstructive. Even on the material plane we see how the vibrations of light and heat penetrate those of visible and tangible substance, and how, in your more recent discoveries, light rays penetrate solid metals formerly called opaque. When I say that these vibrations are interpenetrable and non-obstructive, the statement must be taken as approximating the truth, and not as a finality, independent of all conditions; for by the power of the will, or as a result of mental habit, a man may either exclude or admit to his consciousness the thought vibrations of others. But you may set it down as a fundamental fact that there is nothing or no condition of which the mind can conceive that may not become an objective reality, which is the creative faculty in all of us. This city is here to us just as really and actually as were the trees of Guir forest a short time ago. By opening our inward sight, and putting ourselves in accord with another vibratory plane of existence, we are in full *rapport* with a condition that makes no impression upon the members of the sleeping world not so impressed."

"But we left the house at midnight, and here we are in the broad light of day. Do you mean to tell me that the mind controls the sun itself? The thing is so astounding that I feel as if I were losing my reason."

"And did I not tell you that it was unwise to gratify curiosity in this realm when unprepared by a long course of training? But let me quote you a few words from one of our greatest philosophers"; and Ah Ben quoted the following from Franz Hartman's "Magic, White and Black":

"Visible man is not all there is of man, but is surrounded by an invisible mental atmosphere, comparable to the pulp surrounding the seed in a fruit; but this light, or atmosphere, or pulp, is the mind of man, an organized ocean of spiritual substance, wherein all things exist. If man were conscious of his own greatness, he would know that within himself exist the sun and the moon and the starry sky and every object in space, because his true self is God; and God is without limits."

"These thoughts are utterly beyond me," said Paul uneasily.

"As I told you they would be," replied Ah Ben, turning his chair and looking at his pupil with a kindly expression; and then, with his usual earnestness, he added: "But they will not be so always."

"And you tell me that these things are actually as real as the furniture in Guir House?" inquired Henley.

"Quite!" answered the guide. "Test them for yourself. Do you not see this magnificent dome above our heads, supported upon these wonderful pillars? Try them, touch them, strike them with your hand. Are they not solid? Apply every test in your power to their reality; they will not fail you in one—and, let me ask, what further evidence have you of the furniture of which you speak? Thought is real; and the man who can hold to his thought long enough endows it with objectivity."

"It is a mystery involving mysteries," sighed Paul; "and I could never even ask the questions that are crowding into my mind."

"So it is with all life," the old man replied thoughtfully, pressing his hand against his forehead as he gazed into the brilliant scene without seeming to look at anything especial; "and so it is with all life," he repeated in a minute; "it is a mystery involving mysteries! What are dreams? Give them a little more intensity, as in the case of the somnambule or clairvoyant, and they are real. The trouble is, Mr. Henley, that few of us ever come to realize that life itself is a dream; and when science recognizes that fact, many of the difficulties she now encounters will vanish. Let me repeat a few lines from the Song Celestial, or *Bhagavad Gita*.

"Never the spirit was born; the spirit shall cease to be never;
Never was time it was not; end and beginning are dreams,
Birthless and deathless and changeless remaineth the spirit forever;
Death has not touched it at all, dead though the house of it seems.

"These thoughts are better understood in the East," continued Ah Ben, "where the people give less time to *religion* and more to the *philosophy* of life. And what are dreams but a part of our inner existence? None the less mysterious because we are so familiar with them. There are numerous authenticated records of dreams that have carried a man through an apparently long life, but which have really occupied less than a second of time as counted with us; through all the minutiae and details of youth, courtship, marriage, a military career, war with all its horrors, the details of the last battle where death was inevitable, and where the last shot was fired and heard that brought the great change—of *awakening*, and the sudden perception that the entire phantasmagoria had been caused by the slamming of the door, which the exhausted sleeper had only that second opened as he dropped into a chair beside it. The facts in this case are proven; no perceptible time having elapsed. Time—time is nothing. Time is only what we make it. An hour in a dungeon might be an eternity, while a million years in the Levachan of the Hindoo would seem but a summer's day."

8

Continuing their walk, they followed an avenue of dazzling beauty, which led to a green hill overlooking the town, upon which stood a temple of transcendent splendor. The sunlight flashed upon its marble walls and *chevaux de frise* of minarets. Paul was filled with amazement, and demanded an explanation.

"Let us climb the hill and see for ourselves," answered his guide, leading the way.

Crowds of people passed in and out through the open portals of the temple; and when sufficiently near, Paul read the inscription above the principal entrance:

"*In Commemoration of the Birth of Human Liberty.*"

"I am as puzzled as ever," he declared, with a look of resignation. "It is the most stupendous and remarkable edifice I ever beheld!"

They passed up by a marble terrace and entered the building through an archway so wide and lofty that it might have spanned many ordinary houses. Windows of jeweled glass scattered a thousand tints over walls and columns of barbaric splendor, where encrusted gems of every hue, scintillating with strange fires, were grouped in dazzling mosaics portraying historic scenes in endless pageant. It was a miracle of art and trembling iridescence. White pillars, set with jewels, rose and branched above their heads like the spreading boughs of gigantic trees. The throng of humanity surged hither and thither, and yet so vast was the nave of the temple that nowhere was it crowded. Paul clung closely to his comrade's arm, fearful lest his only friend in this strange world should be lost to him. On they walked; Ah Ben having an air of long familiarity with the scene, while Paul was dazed and bewildered. Occasionally they would stop to examine some object of special interest or to take in with comprehensive view the marvels surrounding them. But the temple was too grand, too glorious for a hasty appreciation of its wonders.

Entering an elevator, they ascended to the roof and stepped out upon a mosaic pavement of transparent tiles. Looking over the parapet, they beheld a country of vast extent, where field, forest, and watercourse combined in a landscape of rare beauty. Beneath lay the marble city with its palaces, parks, and fountains. In the distance were shadowy hills and gleaming lights; and above, a sky whose singular purity was reflected over all. The height was great, but the roof so extensive that it seemed more like some elevated plateau than a part of a building. A multitude of spires rose upon every side like inverted icicles, and Paul was amazed to discover an inscription at the base of each.

"I have a distinct impression of the meaning," he said, looking up at his guide; "but how, I can not tell."

"Yes," answered the old man solemnly, "you now perceive that this stupendous temple commemorates the birth of liberty, or the death of superstitions, and the consequent liberation of the human mind from the slavery of false belief. The temple itself is a monument to the whole, while each minaret commemorates the downfall of some scientific dogma, and the consequent release of the human mind from its thralldom. The limit of man's power over his environment has been extended again and again; and even in your day, Mr. Henley, you have witnessed such marvelous advances as have adduced the aphorism, that this is an age of miracles. We speak from one end of the continent to the other. We sit in New York and sign our name to a check in Chicago. We reproduce a horse race or any athletic sport just as it occurred with every movement to the slightest detail, so that all men can see it in any part of the world at any time quite as well as if present at the original performance. We photograph our thoughts and those of our friends. We reproduce the voices of the departed. We commune with each other without the intervention of wires. We have lately pictured the human soul in its various phases. We see plainly through iron plates many inches in thickness, and look directly into the human body. Our food and precious stones are made in the laboratory, and a syndicate of scientists has recently been formed for the transmutation of the baser metals into gold. When man can produce food, clothing, and all the precious metals at will; when he can see what is occurring at a distance without the necessity of lugging about a cumbersome piece of machinery like his body—when all these and many other discoveries have been brought to perfection, the farmer and manufacturer may cease their labors. The necessity for war will no longer exist, as the righting of wrongs, the acquisition of territory, and the payment of debt will not demand it. But all these things and many more, Mr. Henley, will be brought to perfection before the liberation of man shall have been effected, which will be when he comes to understand that, with proper training and the ultimate development of self-control, there is no limit to his power. As I have told you before, self-control is the secret of all power. The day is not distant when the dogmas of science will be set aside for the spirit of philosophic inquiry. Then men will no longer say that they have reached the goal of human capacity or that they can not usurp the prerogative of the gods, for it will be known that we are all gods!"

Later they descended to the ground and passed into the superb public gardens of the city. Seating themselves beside one of the numerous fountains sparkling with colored waters and perfumed with strange aquatic plants, they watched the brilliant scene that surrounded them. Aerial chariots flashed above, and men, women, and children moved through the air entirely regardless of the law of gravitation. Occasionally a passer-by would nod to Ah Ben, who returned the salute familiarly, as if in recognition of an old friend; but no one stopped to talk.

"And you know some of these people!" cried Paul in astonishment.

"Some of them." But a look of intense sadness had settled upon the old man's face, quite different from anything Henley had seen. For a moment neither spoke, and then Ah Ben, passing the back of his hand across his forehead, said: "Yes, Mr. Henley, I know them, but I am not of them; and as you see, they shun me."

"I can not understand why that should be," answered Paul, who was conscious of a growing attachment for his guide.

"I can not explain; but some day, perhaps, you may know. Let us continue our walk."

Looking up at the marvelous examples of architecture that surrounded them, Paul observed that many of the houses had no windows, and inquired the reason.

"Windows and doors are here only a matter of taste, and not of necessity," answered the elder man; "the denizens of Levachan enter their houses wherever they please without experiencing the slightest obstruction. Likewise light and air are not here confined to special material and apertures for their admission. We are only just beginning to discover some of the possibilities of matter upon our plane of existence. Here these things are understood; for matter and spirit are one, their apparent difference lying in us."

"Yes," said Paul, "and I perceive that the inhabitants move from place to place through the upper atmosphere in defiance of all law!"

"Law, Mr. Henley, is the operation of man's will. Where man through uncounted eons of time has believed himself the slave of matter, it becomes his master. I mean that the belief enslaves him, and not until he has worked his way out of the false belief, will he become free."

They continued their walk through gardens of bewitching beauty, and amid lights so far transcending any previous experience of Henley's that he no longer even tried to comprehend Ah Ben's labored explanations. At last his guide, turning, abruptly said:

"Come, let us return; the time is growing short!"

"Time!" said Henley, with an amused expression. "I thought you told me that time was only a mental condition!"

"True, I did," said Ah Ben, with a return of the same inexpressibly sad look; "but did I tell you that it had ceased to belong to me?"

There was no intimation of reproof, no endeavor to evade the remark; but Paul could not but observe the change in the man's manner as they retraced their steps. Indeed, he was conscious of an overpowering sadness himself, as he turned his back upon the strange scene.

"Come!" said Ah Ben, with authority, leading the way.

They passed up the grand stairway to the terrace, entering the room at the same window by which they had left it, and Ah Ben closed the sash and drew the curtains behind them.

A moment later Paul went to the window and looked out. There was an old moon, and the forest beneath lay bathed in its mellow light. The sudden transition to his former state was no less astounding than the first.

"Which, think you, is the most real," asked the old man, "the scene before us now, or the one we have left behind?"

Paul could not answer. He was revolving in his mind the marvels he had just witnessed. He could not understand how hypnotism could have created such a world as he had just beheld. It was not a whit less tangible, visible, or audible than that in which he had always lived, and he could not help looking upon Ah Ben as a creature far removed from his own sphere of life. How had the man acquired such powers? These and other thoughts were rushing through his mind. Presently his host touched him lightly upon the shoulder, and said:

"Come, let us descend into the hall again, and finish our pipes."

And so they wandered back through the silent house to the old pew by the fire; and Ah Ben, stirring up the embers and adding fresh fuel, said:

"Although it is late, Mr. Henley, I do not feel inclined for bed; and if you are of the same mind, should be glad of your company."

Paul was glad of an excuse to sit up, and so settled himself upon the sofa, absorbed in meditation. The firelight flickered over their faces and the strange pictures on the wall, and the head of Tsong Kapa shone more plainly than ever before. The portraits on the stairs were as weird and incomprehensible as they had appeared on the first night of his arrival; and the old man and the girl, and their strange life, seemed even more deeply involved in mystery than they had upon that occasion. Paul was now beset with conflicting emotions. The gloom of the house was more oppressive than before; and were it not for his sudden and unaccountable affection for Dorothy, he might have left it at once, had it not again been for the vision of splendor and happiness just faded from his sight. He could not bear the thought of losing forever the sensation of life and power and ecstasy just beginning to dawn upon him, when so cruelly snatched away; and but for Ah Ben he knew he should hope in vain for its return. Naturally, his emotions were strong and tearing him in opposite directions. The old man perceiving the depression of spirits into which his guest had fallen, reminded him gently of his warning regarding the shock of occult manifestation to those who were unprepared.

"It is not that so much," answered Paul, "as the regret I feel at having left it all behind. When a man has only just begun to experience the sensation of life—*of real life*—to find himself suddenly plunged back into a dungeon with chains upon his shoulders, you must admit the shock is terrible."

"Do I not know it?" answered the old man feelingly. "The return is far more to be dreaded than the escape into that life which you were at first inclined to call unreal; and yet, Mr. Henley, you must admit that it is difficult to decide the question of reality between the two worlds."

"True," answered Paul; "and yet I know that what I have just seen can be nothing else than a hypnotic vision; it is impossible it should be otherwise, for it has gone—and beyond my power to recall. What amazes me to the point of stupefaction is the marvelous impression of truth with which hypnotism can fill one. I had always imagined the effect was more in the nature of a dream, but this was vivid, sharp, and perfect as the everyday life about me. I am more bewildered than I have words to express."

"And yet," answered Ah Ben, "you still insist that the things you saw were unreal, because, as you say, they were the result of hypnotism. It seems difficult to convince you of what I have already told you, that hypnotism is not a cause of hallucination, but of fact.

You insist that because the minority of men only are subjected to hypnotic tests, the impressions produced must be false. You will not admit that a minority has any claim to a hearing, although their evidence is based upon precisely the same testimony as that of the majority—namely, the five senses. You have no better right to assume that your present surroundings are any more truthfully reported by your senses than those of your recent experience. You see, you hear and touch; did you not do the same in Levachan?"

"I did, indeed," answered Paul, "and with a clearness that makes it the more difficult to comprehend; still, of course, I know that the vision of Levachan was a deception, while this is real!"

"And because you are convinced that a majority of men would see this as you see it. What if it should be proved that you are wrong?"

"That would be impossible," answered Paul.

"You think so, indeed," answered the old man with a strange look in his eyes; "and yet, if you will look above you and about you, you will see for the first time the way in which this old house looks to the great majority of mankind—indeed, to such a vast majority, Mr. Henley—that your individual testimony to the contrary would be regarded as the ravings of a madman. Look!"

Paul lifted his eyes. The roof was gone, and the stars shone down upon him through the open space. About him were rough walls of crumbling stone, rapidly falling to decay; there were no pictures, there were no stairs with their uncanny portraits, there was no great open fire-place with the blazing logs, nor hanging lamp, nor cheery pew—all—all was gone—and nothing but ruin and decay remained, save some bunches of ivy which had climbed above the edge of the tottering wall, outlined dimly in the moonlight. The floor had rotted away, and dank grass and bushes and heaps of stone had filled its place. A pool of water in a distant corner reflected the sky and a star or two, and the dismal croaking of a frog was the only sound he heard. Through the open casements wild vines and stunted trees had thrust their boughs, and beyond were the pines and hemlocks. Paul stood erect, and stared around him in blank amazement. Where was Ah Ben? He too had departed with the rest. Dazed and wondering, Henley sauntered toward the door, or rather to where the door had once stood, now only an open portal of crumbling stone, from the crevices of which grew bushes and a tangled network of vines. Climbing down over a mass of fallen bricks, he wandered out into the grounds. The lawn was buried beneath a confused jumble of rubbish and weeds, and the forest encroached upon its rights. The graveled road was no longer visible, wild grass, moss, and piles of fallen stone having covered it far below. As he looked above, the moon shone through the casement of a ruined window, and an owl hooted dismally from the open belfry. The old house was a wreck, a tottering ruin, from whatever point he looked; and no room above or below seemed habitable. He walked around to see if the blank wall which guarded the secret chamber was still intact. Yes, there it was; it alone remained untouched by the ravages of time or war. The portraits and human remains were probably safe in their hiding place, and Paul shuddered at the thought. What hand had bound them up in that strange old corner to be hid forever from the eyes of men? He had heard no human word, nor was there apparently any shelter where man or woman could live. Presently amid the deep shadows of the forest something moved. It came nearer, and then from beneath the trees walked out into the moonlight. Paul started; but at the same moment a familiar voice spoke to him. It was Ah Ben's.

"Do not let what you see alarm you, Mr. Henley, for it is the first time in which you have perceived Guir House in what you would call its normal state. As you now behold it, the majority of men would see it."

"Then I have been duped ever since my arrival!" exclaimed Paul in a slightly irritated tone.

"Not at all," answered the elder man complacently. "I have simply presented the house to you as it stood a hundred years ago. The impression you have had of it is quite as truthful as the one now before you. Indeed, it is as truthful as the view you now have of yonder star," he pointed to a twinkling luminary in the north; "for time has put out its fires more than a thousand years ago, so that you now behold it as it then was, and not as it is to-night."

"This hypnotism of yours is quite undoing me," answered Paul, passing his hand across his eyes.

"And yet what you now behold is not hypnotism at all, but fact, as the world would call it. It is what the vast majority of all men would see if here to-night. But I perceive that it is troubling you. Let us return to our old place by the fire, and the house as it was a century ago. In that state of the past I think you will find more comfort than in the melancholy ruin before us."

They climbed back over the fallen piles of bricks, stone, and mortar; and then Ah Ben lifted his withered hand, and touching Henley lightly upon the forehead, said:

"And now we are back in our old seats, just as they used to be in the days of yore!"

Paul looked about him. The fire was burning brightly. The pictures had been restored to their places on the walls. The old lamp and the strangely decorated staircase were all restored, just as he had left them a few minutes before. He gazed long and earnestly at the scene around him, and then fixing his eyes upon Ah Ben, helplessly, said:

"If then I am to understand that this is no longer real, but that the old ruin just beheld is the existing fact, might I ask in what part of the wreck you and Miss Guir have been able to fix your abode, for I saw nothing but crumbling walls—a roofless ruin?"

"The question you ask involves a story, and if you care to listen I will tell it to you, although the hour is late and the night far gone."

"I should enjoy nothing more," said Paul.

And the men filled and lighted their pipes, and Henley listened while
Ah Ben told him the following:

9

"In the early settlement of this State, an Englishman by the name of Guir pre-empted a large body of land, near the center of which he erected this house. Although his intention in coming from the old country was to make his permanent home in the colony, his reasons for doing so were quite different from those which usually induce immigration. Guir was an artist, and a man of some means; and his object in colonizing was not so much to cultivate the soil, or to trade with the Indians, or engage in any business enterprise, as to gratify a craving for nature and surround himself with such scenery as he loved to paint. It would be folly to pretend that Guir was a man of ordinary tastes and disposition; for had he been such, he would never have undertaken a journey, with a family of girls, into such a wilderness as Virginia was at that time. No; from the very circumstances of his birth and education, he was unfitted to live with his countrymen; hence his early adoption of the colony as a home for himself, wife, and daughters. This happened a hundred and fifty years ago."

"He was an ancestor of yours, I presume," said Paul, hoping to gain some clew to the man's identity.

"No," answered Ah Ben, "he was not."

"Pardon the interruption," added Paul, fearing he had annoyed the speaker.

"Naturally, in a country without roads, or even wagon trails," continued the old man, without noticing the apology, "it was years before a house of this size could be completed, as every brick and nearly every stick of timber was brought from England. These, of course, were conveyed by water as far as the rivers permitted, the rest of the journey being performed upon sleds drawn by oxen. But it was Guir's hobby, and in the course of a dozen or fifteen years the job was completed, and the house stood as you see it now. Then the owner set himself to work with brush, canvas, and chisel to decorate his home, and make it, according to his ideas, as beautiful and suggestive of his early youth as imaginable. With his own hands, Mr. Henley, he painted most of these pictures, although his three daughters, inheriting his tastes, assisted him. And thus, as the years rolled by, Guir House became more and more a museum of artistic efforts, embracing many unusual subjects, and in every degree of perfection. The broad acres of the estate produced much that was necessary toward the maintenance of life, and what they lacked was supplied once a year from a distant settlement near the coast. As you can readily understand, there were no neighbors, and but occasional visits from the red man, who looked distrustfully upon the pale-face. This feeling became mutual, and trifling acts of hostility on the part of the natives grew both in frequency and magnitude. Depredations upon Guir's fields and cattle were at first ignored, in the effort to maintain peace, but in time it became necessary to resist them. Upon one occasion, a raid upon a distant field was successfully repulsed, with the aid of his wife and three daughters, attired in men's clothing and mounted upon fast horses. The Indians were so completely surprised by the ruse, being apparently attacked by five men, where they had believed there was only one, that they fled, completely routed, nor did they return for several years. Meanwhile, fearing another and closer attack, Guir converted one of the lower rooms of his house into an impenetrable and unassailable place of refuge. The windows were walled up, to correspond with the stonework of the house, leaving no suspicion of there having been once an opening. Likewise the doors were treated, and then carefully plastered both within and without, with the exception of one, which he made anew, to communicate with a private stairway leading from one of the upper bedrooms. This was the only entrance to the dark retreat, and a heavy bolt was placed upon the inside, to be used by the family in case of attack. There was no reason to suppose that a marauding party would ever find the way to this secret chamber, as the entrance was carefully covered by a scuttle in the floor of a dark closet; and the place being thoroughly fire-proof, the family felt unusually secure in the possession of their new retreat."

"I think I have seen the stairway you speak of," said Paul.

"Yes," answered the old man, "it communicates with the closet of your room.

"One day Guir had left his home. He had ridden alone into the distant hills to dispute the range for some cattle with his natural enemy, the red man. The pow-wow had been long and trying, and it was only with the setting sun that he had come to a proper understanding, as he supposed, with the ugly chief who dominated the region about.

"It was midnight when he reached his home. He pounded sharply on the door; but his good wife, who never retired without him, failed to answer the summons. So, after repeated knocks, Guir forced the door and entered. All was dark. An unearthly stillness pervaded the air, and a horrid suspicion forced itself upon him while groping his way forward to secure a light. Finding the chimney, he raked together a few coals, which he blew into a flame, and then, with trembling hands, lighted the candle upon the shelf above. Looking about him, Guir's heart sank. His house had been wrecked. His pictures, the work of years, were scattered in fragments about the floor. The windows were smashed, and the hall starred with broken glass. Not an ornament, not a treasure remained intact. But this he knew was as nothing to the horrible sight which he expected momentarily to greet his eyes. He called aloud to each member of his family, in the failing hope that some one would answer; but no sound broke the awful stillness. Suddenly he bethought him of the secret chamber, and with a wild prayer that his loved ones had been able to reach it in safety, and were still in hiding there, he started down the narrow stairs in search. Reaching the bottom, he found that the door had been wrenched from its hinges and thrown to the ground; and then Guir's heart sank, never to rise again. Stepping across the threshold of the room, candle in hand, a vision of blood swam before his eyes, and the dimly-burning light revealed the horror-stricken faces of his murdered family. Not one was left to tell the tale, but the story pictured before him was unmistakable in every detail. The treacherous natives had first tortured and then butchered them. For a time he stood transfixed with horror, unable to remove his eyes from the awful scene, or his feet from the spot where he had first beheld it; then, with the cry of sudden madness, he threw himself beside the bleeding corpses and lost all consciousness. How long he remained there was problematical, but on awaking Guir was still in the dark, and where he had fallen. At that moment a strange and overpowering desire seized him. He must paint the portraits of his murdered family before it became too late. Had he been sane, such a ghastly thought would never have possessed him; but Guir was crazed, and for days and nights following he worked in that dismal vault, by the light of a smoking lamp, at the task he had set himself, his fired imagination even intensifying the horrors of the grewsome tableau.

"Upon each canvas he depicted the awful countenance which fact and fancy had imprinted upon his brain. Guir painted not only what he saw, but what he imagined he saw—dreadful faces, loaded with torture and despair. When completed, he hung them upon the walls of the room, and then with his own hands bricked up the entrance from within, having first carefully replaced and bolted the door. When Guir had thus entombed himself, he lay down again upon the floor, and then, still a madman, opened a vein in his wrist. The letting of blood may have sobered him or restored his mental equilibrium; for suddenly, with a wild change in his feelings, he bounded to his feet and repented. Again he was in darkness, and could not guess how much time had elapsed since his fatal act. Staggering to the closed doorway, he endeavored to tear away the bricks he had so recently placed there, but the mortar was hardening fast, and he was unable to find his trowel. Groping frantically along the floor, he searched in vain for some tool to open the vault in which he was buried, and then, with the anguish of despair, dropped again upon the ground to await his fate. Thus Guir died, in an agony of remorse, and with the intensest desire to live."

Ah Ben stopped suddenly, and fixed his eyes upon Henley, as if trying to read his thoughts.

"There is one thing in that story that strikes me as very peculiar," observed Paul, returning his host's look with interest.

"And what is that?" answered the old man, his eyes still fixed on Henley's face.

"The fact that you are able to repeat with such circumstantial detail the feelings and actions of a man who died under such peculiar conditions, and quite alone."

"It might indeed appear strange to you, Mr. Henley, but my familiarity with the case enables me to speak with knowledge and accuracy."

"And would you mind telling me how that is possible?" inquired Paul.

"Because I am the man Guir himself; and I have lived on through such ages of agony that I have no longer the will or desire to appear other than as the ancient wreck before you."

Paul started.

"Do you mean to tell me then that I am talking to a ghost?" he cried in dismay.

"As you please, Mr. Henley; but ghosts are not so different from ordinary people—that is, when they have become materialized. I have just now shown you the real condition of this old house, or rather the way in which the majority of men see it. I do not hesitate, therefore, to show you the ghost that haunts it; nor do I object to explaining the dreadful cause of the haunting, or a little of the philosophy of hauntings in general."

Paul looked aghast. Easy enough was it now to comprehend how the man had talked so familiarly of death and the next life after having actually crossed the threshold and passed into the realm of experience. But there was something too real, too natural about this personality to accept the remark as literal. Familiarity with Ah Ben had shown him to be a man. Paul felt sure of it. And yet here were revealed mysteries never dreamed of; one of which was even now producing an occult spell. Henley drew a deep breath in agony of spirit.

After a moment's pause, the old man continued:

"Ghosts, Mr. Henley, are as real as you; and when a spirit returns to earth in visible form, it is the result of some disquieting influence immediately before the death of the body, or, as I might say, previous to the new life. At the hour of physical birth, such influences cause idiocy or such imperfection of the bodily functions that death ensues, and the spirit returns to seek another entrance into the world of matter. When a man dies dominated by some intense earthly desire, his mind is barred against the higher powers and greater possibilities of spirit; his whole nature is closed against their reception, so that he perceives and hopes for nothing save the continuance of that life which has so completely filled his nature. His old environment overpowers the new by the very force of his will; and if this continues, he becomes not only a haunting spirit, but a materialized one, visible to certain people under certain conditions, and compelled to live out his life amid the scenes which had so attracted him. This, Mr. Henley, has been my case. I shall live upon earth, and be visible to the spiritually susceptible, until the strong impression made at the hour of death shall have worn away."

"And the young lady, is she your daughter?" inquired Paul.

"She is my daughter," answered the old man solemnly.

"How comes it, then, that she addresses you by so singular a name?"

"It is the one she first learned to use in infancy. As I partially explained to you, my mother was a Hindoo, while my father was English. The name Ah Ben belongs to the maternal side of my family."

"Another question—more vital than any I have yet asked, because it concerns my own well-being and happiness," continued Paul; "how is it possible that Dorothy can live in a place like this with a being who is only semi-material?

"Because her nature is double, as is mine," answered the old man. "Dorothy, like her sisters and mother, passed out of this life more than a hundred and fifty years ago."

"And did the same causes operate to bring her back to earth?"

Ah Ben became more serious than ever as he answered: "You have touched upon the sorest point of all, and one which requires further elucidation. Sudden and unnatural death has a retarding tendency upon the spirit's progress; but where one has caused his own destruction, the evil resulting is incalculable. I was a suicide; and ten thousand times over had I better have borne all the ills that earth could heap upon me, than have stooped to such folly. For in what has it resulted? A prolonged mental agony, such as you can never conceive; for I have no home in heaven nor earth, but am forced to wander amid the shadows of each world, unrecognized by those either above or below me. Here I am shunned upon every hand, and, as you saw for yourself, I was equally avoided in Levachan. But that is not all; in the ignorance and selfishness of my grief, I yearned for my lost ones with a solicitude, a consuming fierceness and power of will which insanity only can equal. By nature I was intense; and even had I not committed the fatal act, my vitality would have burned itself away with the awful concentration of feeling. But it must be remembered that I was not the only sufferer from this pitiful lack of self-control. The stronger desires and emotions of the living influence the dead—I use the words in their common acceptation for the sake of convenience—and here is where I caused such incalculable injury to my own child; for Dorothy, having entered the spirit world with inferior powers of resistance, fell under the spell I had wrought, and joined me in the haunting of this old house. Here, Mr. Henley, am I, a suicide, justly deserving the punishment I receive; but there is my child, as innocent as the air of heaven, forced to suffer with me, and it is no small part of my chastisement to realize this fact. People fly from us as they would from pestilence, both in this world and the other, although many of the dwellers in the higher state, from their greater knowledge and loftier development, simply avoid us. And we can not criticise their action in either world, for we are not adapted to either state. We are outcasts."

Ah Ben paused for a moment, and then became deeply impressive, as he added:

"Mr. Henley, let the experience of one who has suffered, and who will continue to suffer more than you can possibly understand—let his experience, I say, warn you against the unreasonable yearning for the return of those who have passed on to their spiritual state! Here our eyes are blinded to the blessedness to come, and it is well it is so; for, were it otherwise, the discipline of earth life would be lost, as too monstrous to be endured. No man could submit to the restraints of matter, with the power and freedom of spirit in sight. If once I could have realized the dreadful results entailed upon what I had lost, by my effort to recover it, I would have known that the blackest curse would have been trifling by contrast. Let the dead rest! and let one who knows persuade you that their entrance into spirit life is a time rather for rejoicing than regret!"

"And is Dorothy to suffer as you have suffered, for what was no fault of hers?" demanded Paul.

"Yes," said Ah Ben; "the law of Karma is the law of nature and the law of God; and while ordinarily she would have passed safely on in the possession of her new-born powers, the pitfall which I blindly laid beset her unwary feet, and she fell. There is but one course open; but one way in which Dorothy can reach either heaven or earth, by a shorter road than that which I am compelled to travel. It is simple, and yet one which, under the circumstances, is almost impossible to achieve; and this from the fact that it requires the cooperation of a human being."

"I should imagine that any one with the ordinary feelings of humanity would gladly do what he could to assist such an unhappy fellow-creature!" exclaimed Paul.

"But she is not a fellow-creature," urged the old man.

"True, but I understood you to say that she might become one with the cooperation of a human being."

"I did," Ah Ben replied; "but where is that to be found?"

"Not knowing the nature of the task, it would be difficult to say," answered Paul, "but I will adhere to my first proposition, that one with the ordinary feelings of humanity would gladly do what he could."

"Mr. Henley, have you the ordinary feelings of humanity?"

"I hope so," answered Paul.

"Would you be willing to marry a ghost, and be haunted for the rest of your life; for the ghost would be sure to outlive you?"

Paul started.

"I have put the case too strongly," continued Ah Ben; "Dorothy is not a ghost in the ordinary sense. She is a materialized spirit, and that, my dear friend, is exactly what you are, with this difference: you have practically no control over your body; while she, having returned from the summer land abnormally, can, like myself, become invisible at will; but, upon the other hand, she is not always visible, even to those whom she would like to have see her. In short, as I have told you before, we belong to neither one world nor the other. But through union with a human creature, Dorothy can once more assume the functions of mortality, and after another period of earth life, become fitted again for the land of spirits."

"I understand you entirely," answered Paul, "and can say, without hesitation or reservation, that I love your daughter, and, be she whom or what she may, will gladly marry her, if she can say as much for me."

"I thought I could not be mistaken in my man," answered Ah Ben. "I have believed in your frankness, honor, and courage from the beginning; and although you came to this house with the intention of deceit, I feel sure that in the more serious situations of life you are to be relied upon. You have spoken to Dorothy, Mr. Henley, and I am confident she shares my trust in you."

"I hope so," answered Paul.

"I know it," the old man replied; "and let me tell you further that this match is not one subservient to the ends of utility or profit; for, were such the motive, the very end would be defeated. Dorothy must love the man she marries, with all her heart and soul; and you can readily understand, ostracized as we are, how difficult it has been to find such a one. For more than a century we have sought in vain, and I have pressed every opportunity and strained every power to bring about such a meeting and such a result as I trust will shortly follow; but the world has given us no chance, and those few who have been able to see us have only fled in terror!"

"Am I at liberty, then, to prove my devotion to your daughter by asking her to marry me?"

"You have already done so," replied Ah Ben, "and I have already given my consent; but I warn you, Mr. Henley, that in your intercourse with my daughter you should remember that you are dealing with a nature far more intense, and with far greater capacity to love, than any you have ever known. While the most fervid desire of Dorothy's life has doubtless been to meet some creature with whom she might affiliate, I believe she would forego even that happiness if convinced that it would prove disastrous to the object of her affection."

Paul extended his hands to Ah Ben, who took them with fervor. "Dear old man!" he said, "although I am speaking to a ghost, I am not afraid of you; and knowing how much you have suffered, it shall be my aim to help and comfort you; for have you not shown me how close is the other world, and so in a measure removed the dread of death? How truly do I feel that those who have left us may be close around us, although we can not see them."

And then, with a new light on all that surrounded him, Paul bade Ah
Ben good-night, and went to his room.

10

The following morning, Mr. Henley was puzzled, in thinking over the conversation of the previous night, to remember that he had not been alarmed at the revelations which Ah Ben had made. The things he had seen and the words he had heard were amazing, but they had not terrified him; and when he recalled the easy and natural manner in which he had talked, he attributed the fact to the same mental change whereby he had perceived the visions.

The breakfast room was deserted, neither Dorothy nor Ah Ben being present; and so Paul partook of the meal alone, which he found prepared as usual. He lingered over his second cup of tea in the hope that the young lady would join him; but after loitering quite beyond the usual hour, he sauntered out into the garden, trusting to find her there. But Dorothy was nowhere to be seen, and Henley sank dejectedly into the old rustic bench to await her coming.

An hour passed, but no token of a human being was in evidence; not even the voice nor the footstep of a servant had been heard, and Paul sat consuming cigarettes at a rate that showed clearly his impatience. At last he returned to the house, and going to his room took pen and paper and wrote, in a large hand:

Will Miss Guir kindly let me know at what hour I may see her? I shall await her answer in the garden.

PAUL HENLEY.

Not being able to find a servant, he took this downstairs and suspended it from the hanging lamp by a thread, and then returned to the garden to tramp up and down the neglected paths, between the boxwood bushes, and to burn more cigarettes. He had not the slightest hope of finding Ah Ben, as that individual never put in an appearance until the day was far spent—in fact, not generally until after the shadows of evening were well advanced; and the only servant he had seen was the dumb boy alluded to, and even he had only appeared occasionally. Clearly there was nothing to do but wait. But waiting brought neither Dorothy nor Ah Ben, and Paul began to wonder seriously where his hosts could have taken themselves. The time wore on, and the shadow of a tall fir showed that the hour of noon had passed. Had he been left in sole possession of this old mansion, whose history was so amazing, and yet whose very existence appeared mythical? He wandered back into the house, and passing through the hall, stopped suddenly. His note was gone. Surely it had been taken, for it could not have fallen. Examining the lamp, Henley saw that a short end of the thread was hanging, indicating that it had been broken and the note carried away. Some one had passed through the building since he had left it. Could it have been the girl? and if so, why had she avoided him? One thing appeared certain; she would know where to expect his letters, and he would now write another. In twenty minutes he had prepared the following, which, having sealed, he again suspended from the lamp in the hall:

DEAREST GIRL—I have waited all the morning to see you, and am growing fearfully impatient. Is it business or pleasure that keeps you away? Why not tell me frankly just what it is, as I can not bear to think that I am avoided from indifference, or because you are getting tired of me. Have I outstayed my welcome at Guir House? I entreat you to give me an answer and an interview, as I am so lonely without you; just how lonely I will tell you when we meet.

PAUL.

Having left this dangling from the same thread, he went out for a walk; and thinking it possible that he might meet Ah Ben in the forest, went in that direction.

The leaves were now falling rapidly, and the clear sky was visible through the bare limbs above; and the open spaces were beginning to give the woods quite a wintry aspect. Guir House was visible from a greater distance than he had ever seen it, and Paul sat down upon a fallen log to take in the picture of the quaint old mansion, buried in the depths of a trackless, almost impenetrable forest. He sang a verse of a familiar song in a loud voice, with the hope of attracting attention, but the distant echo of the last words was the only response that he got. Then he threw himself upon the ground and whistled and smoked alternately, his anxiety constantly growing; but the gentle sighing of the wind in the tree tops, and the uncertain rustling of the leaves, were but poor comfort. Was this to be the end of his strange visit? Was he to start back upon his homeward journey without an opportunity to bid his phenomenal hosts good-bye? He could not bear the thought. Dorothy at all events must be found. He would search the grounds and ransack the house. Surely she must be somewhere within reach of his voice. But then she was so strange, so different from any woman he had ever known. How could he tell, perhaps she had left the old place forever! Henley had not realized until now what a deep and overpowering dependence had suddenly developed in him toward these people. They seemed to hold the key to another world in a more practical and tangible way than he had ever deemed it possible for any mortal-appearing man to do. Even to be shut out from the wonderful city of Levachan would be an overwhelming loss, and how could he ever hope to see it again without their aid? To be deprived forever of the spiritual influence of these eccentric, half-earthly acquaintances was a thought he could not tolerate. Even the horrors through which they had passed appeared trivial as compared with the glimpses they had afforded him of happiness. But to see these things—to feel the mystery of their power and beauty just beginning to descend and take possession of him—and then to be snatched back to earth, with the inability to return, was too horrible, and like the ecstatic visions of a drowning man cut short by rescue. While he had Ah Ben and Dorothy within his reach, he felt the possibility of return; but suddenly they had gone, and for the first time he realized what they had been to him. Then it began to dawn upon him what these people must have suffered in a century and a half, and what they must continue to endure for untold time to come, in their inability to return in full to that world they had left, or even to take part in the affairs of this. Surely their case was far worse than his, for after a few years he would be freed from the bondage of matter, and would grapple with the mysteries which had become so fascinating; but with them it was different. Unfitted for either world, without a friend and alone, they must drag out their weary existence until the law of Karma was satisfied. But he would not give them up; he could not; for were they not the new life, the new atmosphere, the very essence of his newly discovered self? He had felt, and seen, how possible it was for a man to tread on air—to walk the upper regions of the sky, and he could never again be contented to crawl upon the surface of the ground like a worm. But without Ah Ben he must crawl. With him, Paul felt that all things were possible, which powers he felt that Dorothy also possessed; though, alas, through the crime, and earth-bound cravings of his host, these powers had been sadly curtailed.

Nerveless and dispirited he returned to the garden gate. Some one had been there since he had passed, for there were fresh footprints along the walk, of a small, feminine type, and directed toward the forest. The steps had passed outward, and their track was lost in the leaves beyond. Surely Dorothy had left the house and gone for a ramble in the woods without having seen him. How could he have missed her, and could it have been intentional, were thoughts which came unpleasantly to Paul at that moment. He stood gazing long and earnestly in the direction taken by the departing footsteps, and doing so, his attention was attracted by the flight of a bird which came swooping towards him from the depths of the woodland glade. Nearer and nearer it came, uttering a strange, shrill cry, as if to attract his attention; and then, after circling in the air above his head, came fluttering down, and lighted upon the gate-post at his elbow. It was Dorothy's parrot. But what did it mean by this unusual freak of familiarity? Paul spoke to the bird, which pleased it; and when he put out his hand to smooth its feathers, the parrot lifted its wings, and with a loud cackle exhibited a note which had been carefully tied beneath one of them. Henley relieved the animal of its burden, and discovered that the note was addressed to himself. When he looked around again, the parrot had flown away. This is what the note contained:

GUIR HOUSE.

MY OWN DEAR COMRADE—I call you my own because you are all that I ever had, but even now the memory of our few brief interviews is all that is left to me, for I must go without you. So happy was I when we first met, that I don't mind telling you, since we shall not meet again, how, in anticipation, I rested in your dear arms and felt your loving caresses; for you were all the world to me then—the only world I had ever known—and the break of day seemed close at hand. But soon the thought of drawing you down into that awful abyss 'twixt heaven and earth, which has whirled its black shadows about me for more than a century, seized me, and I could not willingly make a thrall of the one I loved; and so I leave you to those for whom you are fitted, while I shall continue my solitary life as before. You say that you are lonely without me! But what is your loneliness to mine? I, who never had a comrade; who never felt the joy of friendship; and who was dazed with the sudden flush of love, of hunger satisfied, of companionship! Have you ever felt the want of these, dear Paul? Have you ever known what it is to be alone—to live in an empty world—and that, not for a time, but for ages? Yes, you will say, you understand it, and that you pity me, and yet you do not know its meaning; for you at least can live out the life for which God and nature have fitted you, while I am fit for nothing. You know not what it is to be shunned; to be avoided; to be feared! You go your way, and smile and nod to those you meet, and they are pleased to see you. You are welcome among your friends, as they to you. Live on in that precious state, and feel blessed and happy, for there are worse conditions, although you know it not.

And now I am going to tell you a strange thing. It is this: I have shadowed your life from the hour of your birth. I have watched your career, and where able have guided and helped you, knowing that you were one whom I could love. I have helped to make you what you are, and therefore my right of possession is doubly founded, even though my love be too great to lead you astray. Gradually I led you up to the hour when all was ripe, and then mentally impressed you with the letter which you thought you received, and which I knew would affect you through your strongest characteristics—love of adventure, and—curiosity—as well as from the fact that you were susceptible to mental influence. You came, and I was happy—more happy than you will ever know—until my unsated Karma thwarted my plan, and showed that while seeking my own peace, I might possibly endanger yours. That ended all. I could go no further. But even now, as before, I shall come to you in spirit, during the still hours of night; for my love is more intense and strangely different from that which waking men are wont to feel. It is that which sometimes comes in dreams. Do you not know what I mean?

You will feel bewildered on reading this, and at a loss to understand many things, but remember that your inward or spiritual sight has been opened through the power of hypnotism, and you must not judge things as in your normal state.

When you reached our little station of Guir, you were expecting to find me there, and expectation is the proper frame of mind in which to produce a strong impression; and therefore, although you did not know what I was like, Ah Ben and I together easily made you see me as I was, together with the cart and horse; and although you actually got into the stage which was waiting, you thought you were in the cart with me. The incident of the broken spring was merely suggested as a fitting means to bring you back physically from the coach to the cart, where for the first time, in the moonlight, you saw me in semi-material form, visible as a shadow to some men, but wholly so to you. Had I appeared thus at the station, I should have alarmed all who saw me, and so I came to you only. The two worlds are so closely intermingled that men often live in one while their bodies are in another, and to those who are susceptible, the immaterial can be made more real than the other. I know these things, because, while at home in neither, I have been in both.

And now, dear comrade, think sometimes of her who loves you, and to whom you have been the only joy; and she will be with you always, although you may not know it, except in your dreams.

One more word. Think happily of the dead, for they are happy, and in a way you can not understand. If you love them truly, rejoice that they have gone, for what you call their death is but their birth, with powers transcending those of their former state, as light transcends the darkness. Disturb them not with idle yearnings, lest your thought unsettle the serenity of their lives. Let the ignorance which has ruined me be a warning. Some day I shall complete my term of loneliness, and begin life anew. We will know each other then, dear Paul, as here. Remember, I shall always be your spirit guide. DOROTHY.

Henley folded the letter and looked about him in bewilderment, and with a sense of loneliness he had never known before. He thought he could realize the emptiness of life, the dissociation with all things, of which Dorothy had spoken. He was adrift, without anchor in either world. Heart-broken and crushed, he determined to find the girl at all hazards, and bounded down the garden path in search of Ah Ben, who alone could help him. At the last of the boxwood trees he stopped, and then, *in an agony of horror, beheld the roofless ruin of the old house as Ah Ben had shown it to him.* The crumbling walls and broken belfry, half hidden amid the encroaching trees, were all that was left of Guir House and its spacious grounds. Heaps of stone and piles of rubbish beset his path, and the open portals, choked with wild grass and bushes, showed glimpses of the sky beyond. In a panic of terror lest his reason had gone, Paul flew madly on in the direction from which Dorothy had first brought him. But not an indication of what once were ornamental grounds remained. Beyond, an unbroken forest was upon every side, and the growth was wild and dense. On he rushed, with both hands pressed tightly against his head, neither knowing nor caring whither he went. But at last two shadowy forms emerged from a dense thicket of calmia upon his left, and Paul felt that their influence was kindly, and that they had come to guide him back into the world he had left behind.